Back Cc

Unbeknownst to her, Maddy has an enemy who wants to kill her. Greyback is determined to protect her, even if he has to kidnap her to do it.

Maddy hasn't had the best of luck. She was found on the steps of a church as a baby, then her adoptive parents died in a car crash and she spent years in foster care. Now she finds herself being kidnapped by a sexy man with a six-pack named Greyback.

Grey claims to have known her birth parents. He also claims to be a lion shifter. Oh, and he says she's his mate. And if all that wasn't enough, he also claims there's someone out there—an ex-pack member—who wants to kill her.

Can Greyback keep Maddy safe, and will they find love in the process?

Content Warning: contains strong language, some violence, and lots of hot, steamy sex scenes

Chapter 1

The callused hand over Maddy's mouth muffled any scream she could have let out.

"Don't scream and I won't hurt you," the deep male voice behind her whispered in her ear.

Yeah, right! Was this where she was to die? The shitty life she had led was going to end here just as she was beginning to land on her feet and make her way in the world!

She had finished work late because her smarmy boss had wanted his report typed before she left. She was so tired she'd decided to take a shortcut against all her self-preservation, feelings and actions she had used all her life. She had cut through an alley so she could get home sooner rather than later.

Yeah, sod's law for you!

Breathing through her nose, which the male had graciously left unsealed, she could smell his skin when she inhaled. Should she be thinking he smelled fucking good in the predicament she was in? He smelled of wood, grass, and nature.

She nodded in response to the man's order not to scream, while all the time trying to think of ways to escape his other arm that was grasped firmly around her waist.

"Not that I don't trust you," he sniggered, "but we're going to take this very slowly. Slip off your shoes first."

She did as he told her. This dropped her height six inches. She could feel him lower his body slightly to match hers. However, even that still left her head now resting on his shoulder.

"Now drop your bag on the ground."

She did as he asked with a frown. Everything she needed was in that bag, including the ever-present and needed pen knife.

"I am faster and stronger than you, and there is no way you can outrun me. If I have to run after you, I will spank that arse of yours 'til it shines, hear me?"

Anger rose inside her. She'd been in many situations she hadn't wanted to be in. Problems like this seemed to find her, but as she grew older and more experienced she found ways to deal with the shit she was dealt. She knew she needed to think clearly in order to get out of this situation, but with her fiery temper it was difficult. Her anger had been the one thing she had never really managed to control. Although, at times it was also what got her out of a bad position.

She nodded with a mantra of SING going through her head. *Solar plex. In-step. Nose. Groin.*

She found herself whipped around and scooped up in muscled arms and pulled across a well-built chest.

"I've watched you for a while now, and I know what you're thinking. Not a chance, little one."

What the hell? Watched? By whom? Whose fucking radar had she spiked?

She tried to struggle against his arms and chest. Her arm that wasn't trapped between their bodies began to flail, looking for anything to punch, pinch, stab, but it was grabbed and hugged tight to her body. She couldn't even move her legs as they too were tightly held. She looked at his face, making sure that if she were to come out of this alive she could identify the jerk. He had long blond hair to his shoulders, plump lips, and a wide nose. He had blond, bushy eyebrows over amber eyes. His jaw looked strong and square. Seeing him look down challengingly at her she stared back in defiance.

The man began to walk across the street, toward a waiting black van. In the reflection of the dark paint she watched as he carried her with such grace his body didn't even look like he was lifting her, and she wasn't exactly stick thin and light, she had generous curves being she loved food and hated working out. Exercise was something she didn't much care for. If people couldn't accept her as she was, screw them.

She could see her house over the top of the van. *I was so close to it.* As she opened her mouth to scream, his mouth came down on hers.

Crap. Yes, she was in trouble!

Why don't I feel more frightened?

Why am I letting this guy kiss me?

Her toes curled as his tongue slid along her lips. She caught the aftertaste of mint. He deepened the kiss, making her pussy twitch, shooting electric shocks through to her clit. Her body relaxed against his as again his scent began to flow over and around her. Her fuzzy mind forgot to scream and shout to draw attention. Her traitorous mind obliterated any thought of fighting, and her body melted against the man carrying her away from everything she knew.

She heard the van door open and another deep voice from inside pulled her out of her stupor.

"Hole in one, Alpha. Nice catch!"

Her mind began clearing, and she started to shove against the man's chest and tried to kick out with her legs, but he just ducked and climbed into the back of the van without any fuss. He growled at the other bloke in the van he reached out to grab her. As the man holding her sat down and adjusted her so she was sitting on his lap, the other man slapped his hand on the inside of the van a couple of times and sat down in the seat in front of them while sliding the door shut. Within seconds the van's engine started and the vehicle moved forward. Full-blown awareness kicked in, Maddy wasn't making it home tonight…if ever.

"What do you want? 'Cause you just left all my money in that bag on the ground."

She received no answer.

"Are you going to rape me?" she managed to ask, feeling what she assumed was the man's rather impressive erection under her butt. Maybe if she ground against him hard enough she could hurt him and he might let her go, but then she'd have to cope with the other bloke and get out of the van. And her captor was a huge man, so there was a major chance he'd hurt her back in a big way. Looking around, she sighed heavily.

"Little one, however much I would like to thrust my cock into you over and over I would only do it if you were willing. I'm not into rape." He looked sternly down at her with his bright amber eyes.

"I have to get back to my kid. His babysitter will be worried and call the cops. I won't say anything—"

"You don't have a kid."

"My mother…she needs her medication."

"You're a foster kid, you don't know your parents."

Her frustration was growing at being thwarted from getting away. Just how much did this man know about her? With a last feeble attempt, she tried one more thing. "My cat needs to be fed."

He brought his face down directly in front of hers so she could smell the slight mint on his breath as he spoke. "No kids, no parents, no fucking pets! You live on your own and have done so for years. You don't even have any friends who will miss you. Now stop talking and wait 'til we get where we're going and all will be explained. No one will hurt you, unless…" He lifted an eyebrow. "…you want that spanking!"

She looked into his eyes, she'd never seen such a captivating color, they were dark amber and seemed to glow with mirth. *How dare he?*

"Jerk!" She turned her head and pretended to examine the side of the van.

Chapter 2

Maddy was finally in his arms. Greyback couldn't believe it—after all these years she was there, on his lap, wiggling her cute behind on his hard-as-rock cock. He couldn't wait to be inside her, to see her swell with his cubs. He closed his eyes briefly, summoning all his strength to calm his wayward dick.

The animal inside him growled at his human half, the beast wanted him to roll her over and mate her there and then. *Better to ask for forgiveness than permission.*

Maddy's scent slowly filled the confined area, not helping his raging hard-on at all. He ran his hand up and down her arm every now and again, wanting to feel as much bare skin as he could. He was glad she had a little weight on her, something to hold onto while he fucked her hard. He couldn't hold the groan in as thoughts of him pounding into her flooded his brain.

He looked down at the woman in his arms and wondered how she was going to take the fact he knew all about her. She was soon to receive a history lesson on herself. He winced. He didn't think it was going to go well.

She wore a pinstriped jacket and skirt that hugged her generous curves, and her long blonde hair was pulled up into a ponytail on the top of her head. She had a pert little nose. Her lips were still nicely swollen from when he had kissed her before.

He ran his tongue along his lips, enjoying the residue of her on them. He smiled, watching her wiggle her cute little toes in aggravation. Oh, she had fire inside her, he liked that, and she was going to need it. After a while her body relaxed against his as her exhaustion took over. Her beautiful aqua-colored eyes closed, and she slipped into an anxious sleep. A little while later her body twisted in his arms, curling up against his chest. Resting his head on top of hers, he too closed his eyes, taking comfort in the fact that she was in his arms, safe. For now, at least.

Greyback knew Maddy was in for a shock. He was going to have to explain how a pride of thirty shifter lions that he was Alpha of lived in Britain but were never seen. Well, apart from one small incident a few years back that could have been potentially dangerous. A teen, after an argument with his father, had gone into town. He still hadn't been able to fully control the strong beast inside him and had shifted. A photo of his lion had hit the front page of the newspaper the next day. Luckily, with the police not finding any other lions in the area it was put down as a photoshop incident.

He was so engrossed in his thoughts and enjoying his mate on his lap he was surprised when Mace, his beta, gave him a shake. "Grey, we're here."

Mace had been there from the beginning. After they'd finally tracked the female down Mace had spent the next few months being her shadow. With the help of others in his pride they had found out as much as they could about her life. Tonight they had gone to pick her up, bring her home, and explain everything to her. It was pure luck she had walked through that alley, making the plan a whole lot easier.

Grey looked down at the still sleeping bundle in his arms. Climbing out of the van, he walked behind Mace to his house. They lived in a quiet, wooded area in the west of England. The land had been in his family for years. It was heavily warded thanks to the shaman, Amier. At one time several mystics lived among his people but Jerrick, his father's beta, had lost his mind, causing a lot of problems. This left only one now and she remained in seclusion.

"Grey?" Mace looked at him, as if waiting for an answer.

"Huh, what?"

His beta chuckled and shook his head in exasperation. "Having the female is already getting to you, Alpha? Do you want me to stick around?" he asked slowly in a mocking manner.

"No," Grey growled. "Go see your mate. Give her a peck from me."

The beta replied with his own snarl and left to go home to his family.

Grey gently placed his precious bundle on his king-size bed, then he carefully pulled off her jacket and tossed it on a nearby chair. Stripping down to his t-shirt and boxers, he lay next to her and pulled the covers over them both. He needed to grab a quick cat-nap, because tomorrow was going to be a long day. He wasn't worried his mate would get far if she woke up before him, because he was a light sleeper. Taking one last look at her, he wrapped an arm over her waist and closed his eyes.

* * * *

Maddy tried to move her head but her face was stuck to the cushion under her head. Sighing, she wiggled and confirmed she was fully dressed. She must have fallen asleep on the couch again. She lay there for a few seconds, trying to remember what day it was when the pillow beneath her head inhaled deeply and purred. *It did what?*

"Oh my God. Shit!" She bounded up, her eyes opening in shock, and caught a glimpse of a man with blond hair and amber eyes staring at her as she fell off the bed butt-first with her legs tangled in the sheets.

She was cursing a blue streak, trying to free herself from the blasted material when his head popped over the edge of the bed and he looked down at her.

"Having trouble there, little one?"

"You…you stay away from me." She scrabbled across the carpeted floor away from the bed and its bloody coverings. "You slept with me? I mean I slept with you? Shit, what the hell?" She shook her head, trying to remember what had happened. She didn't drink so that couldn't be it. Then it all came to her in a rush. "You took me…in a van… Where are we? Stupid question really, you're not going to tell me. What do you want? You can answer that, right?"

She looked around then back at the man who was watching her from the huge four-poster bed. The room was manly, strong oak furniture, brown and beige colors. Nothing in the room spoke to her that said *hi, I have a female here*. Something above her caught her eye, and she saw the reflection of the male lying on the bed. *Fucking hell, he has a mirrored ceiling.* Her gaze moved back to the male in question, and his lips lifted in a smirk.

"Morning, Maddy. Do you wish for me to answer your questions now? The floor is a rather uncomfortable place to have an early morning conversation. Maybe I can tempt you into having some breakfast. I throw a mean full English together, and my coffee isn't the cheap kind either." He raised his eyebrows in question.

Maddy pulled herself together, getting to her feet. "Breakfast? Coffee? You kidnapped me, you stole me away to here—wherever that may be—slept next to me, then ask me if I want breakfast? Are you crazy?" She moved toward the bedroom door and grasped the handle to open it. "No, don't answer that. I don't want to know." Opening the door, she walked out into a long hallway.

"The bathroom is on the left," he shouted.

With her bladder screaming in protest at being full she decided that the bathroom would be the first move, then find a way out. She examined the room while relieving herself, searching for ways to escape. There were small windows on the two outside walls, but they were so high up she wouldn't have a chance of getting through them. Shaking her head, she flushed and washed her hands.

Opening the door, she listened only to hear the crackle and hiss of what could be a frying pan coming from the far end of the hallway. Walking toward it, she opened another of the doors on the way. It was another bedroom, which was smaller than the one she'd woken up in. But it was the floor-to-ceiling window that held her attention. Although all she could see was trees, it was a way out. Quietly, she shut the door, walked toward the window, opened the clasp, and slipped through it.

"Going somewhere, princess?" The man's deep, rolling voice went through her.

With a scream she turned, startled to see… "Just what is your name?" she asked, gathering her senses together.

"Greyback, but most of my people call me Grey. Now would *you* like to answer my question?"

"Your parents named you Greyback?" *Well, he is the size of a gorilla.*

"My grandfather did actually," he said, puffing his chest out in pride. "Answer. My. Question."

"I was taking a breath of fresh air." She placed her hands on her hips in a challenge. *Yeah, go ahead, punk, make my day.*

"Breakfast is this way." He gestured her forward around the cabin's wraparound porch.

Fine, food first then escape.

They went inside to the kitchen and she took a seat at the breakfast bar. She watched him cook as she drank the exquisite coffee he had put in front of her.

"Well, you haven't raped or killed me yet, and you made me a good breakfast, which may be my last one. Are you going to tell me exactly why I've been kidnapped and taken to the middle of nowhere?" Through the cabin windows all she saw was tree after tree. Wherever this was, it sure had a lot of woods.

Chapter 3

Grey watched Maddy sniff at the breakfast he placed in front of her. "I didn't poison it," he smirked.

As she tucked in, he started telling her story.

"You were found on the steps outside a small church in Wittering, Cambridge. The woman who played the church organ found you, and you were named after her. After an extensive investigation where no parents were located you were placed up for adoption." He watched her push the half-eaten breakfast away from her. "You were two when Donald and Penelope Kade were killed in a car crash. They had no family that could take you in, so you spent several years being shipped from foster parents to children homes. When you were fifteen you ran away from your last foster home after an altercation with another foster kid."

He paused, waiting to see if she added to the story. He knew the reason for the fight, being one of his pride had talked to the now man in question, but he wanted her to tell the story. But when she reminded silent, he continued.

"We lost track of your whereabouts for about five years until you popped up after registering for a college course. You lived with Frannie Plad, an elderly woman who had no family of her own, for the entire course while working several jobs at the same time. After she died you squatted in her place until you raised enough money to get your own one-bedroom apartment where we picked you up."

"Where you kidnapped me," she snapped.

Ignoring her, he continued. "After finishing your college course you managed to get a secretary job, where you were working for a slimeball who liked to caress your arse as you walked past. I actually wonder just how long you would have put up with him."

Maddy stood up and started clapping her hands. "Well done. Bravo. You know all about my life." She stopped to place a hand on a cocked hip. "Do I get to know why now?"

Standing to put a little height over the sassy woman, he replied, "I know about your natural parents."

He watched all her pluckiness drop from her persona.

* * * *

My parents? No fucking way! She'd been left in a white blanket on some church steps twenty-three years ago. No one knew where she had come from.

"My real parents? Yeah, yeah. Give the poor orphan a lollipop then take it away from her. Screw you, buddy, and the horse you rode in on."

Turning, Maddy ran for the door. She managed to grab hold of the handle and swing the door open before once again she was swept off her feet and carried over the caveman's shoulders. This time the jerk didn't have hold of her hands, so clenching her fists, she swung as hard as she could and pounded on his back. After a few good punches she found herself thrown down and landing in a sitting position on the leather couch. She kicked out at him, but he caught her ankles. When she pushed them to the floor she punched at him, but this time he caught her wrists and held them against her knees. Geeze, he had huge paws.

"Calm," he barked. "I *do* know who your parents were."

"Were?"

"Yes, were." He didn't release her hands. She wasn't sure at that particular time if she wanted him to.

"I'm listening."

"First I have to tell you a little about me and the pride."

"Pride?"

"Yes, pride. The Tranquil Hunters Pride. We are a group of people who live close to each other—"

She blew out a breath in frustration and interrupted him, shaking her head and rolling her eyes. "Here we go…come join our group, we will look after you…"

"Enough," he growled. "Listen to me." He walked to a bookcase and pulled out a photo album. Bringing it back to where she sat, he shoved the open book into her hands. "Your parents. May and Trevor Compton."

Looking down at the open page before her she saw two people smiling back at her. She had always wondered how she would feel if she happened to find her parents. How would she cope? Would her parents love her? And if so, could she forgive them for abandoning her and love them in return? Looking at the photo, she saw some similarities, like the woman's features and the male's eyes, but she felt nothing. Numb. Pulling the photo from the book, she held it between her shaking fingers, hoping for some kind of emotion. Anything. Dropping both the photo and book on the floor, she looked up at Grey. She suddenly found her emotion—pure and utter anger.

"I don't want to listen to any more. Those people may look similar, but they are nothing to me. Even if they were my parents, I don't feel anything but anger. They left me on church steps in the middle of nowhere. You kidnap me, bring me to this god-forsaken place, tell me my life fucking history, and then expect me to believe you know about my parents. Listen to me, jerk face, no one knows them. I didn't have anything on me when they found me, not even a fucking note. Even if you did know them, why the hell am I only finding out now? I was in the newspapers and on the television when they found me, someone could have come forward then." Standing up, she stomped her feet, letting some of the anger she'd felt all her life at being abandoned roar through her, and then she screamed to release some more.

Pure shock reeled through her when she found herself lifted and placed over his knees. Her tight work suit skirt ripped up the back, leaving her backside feeling fresh air. She howled as his hand came down on her butt several times. Tears flowed freely, falling on the floor beneath her head.

"Are you going to hear me out?" he asked, halting after the fourth spank. Her arse burned.

"Jerk," she shrieked at him, not ready to give in.

Slap.

Filling her lungs with air, she let out another scream of pure frustration and annoyance and then slumped over his legs, grief, sadness, and pain hitting her all at once. Why had she been left? Why did everyone leave her?

"Okay, arsehole, I give in," she whispered, sobbing.

Her whole world twisted and turned again until she was sitting—on her very sore butt—on his lap. *He just spanked me like a fucking naughty child.* Anger bloomed deep inside her, but it couldn't stop the tears as they leaked down her face. He didn't say anything, just held her and cooed gently until her sobs finally began to stop.

"I'm not a child, you know," she grumbled.

He carried on talking about her life as if she hadn't just cursed the shit out of him and he hadn't spanked her like a child. She sat in stunned silence, listening.

"First, let me explain about the Tranquil Hunters. We are one of three lion shifter groups in Britain."

"Come on…lion shifters? Bullshit!"

"Are you going to listen?" he growled. His amber eyes flickered to a lighter amber and the shape became elongated.

"Yes, I'll listen," she squeaked out. A little belief began creeping in.

"Your parents lived with our group for many years. Your mother was a soothsayer, and your father was a shaman who managed the wards around our property. A year before you were born your mother predicted that their one and only daughter would be my mate, along with the fact she would be powerful in her own right."

Looking up at him, she could feel the truth in his words. She had always had a gift of knowing when the truth was told or not. Rolling her eyes, she realized her life was heading further into the twilight zone.

"I was four at the time. My parents, although they were dubious, accepted that this may happen. However, Jerrick, my father's beta, didn't take it well. He and his mate had a two-year-old daughter. She and I were very close, which had him believing we were mates. He became unpredictable, unstable, letting his jealousy overcome him. It was a hard time for my father. He watched his closest friend, someone who'd had his back and trust for so long, come apart. He knew the day would come when he would have to do something about it. When your parents announced they were pregnant it sent him over the edge."

She watched the man holding her take a deep breath and close his eyes. She could feel the sadness come from him in waves.

"Your mother foresaw that Jerrick would attack them, and she went to my father and informed him. Once confronted, Jerrick denied it, and without proof my father couldn't do anything, he could only watch and wait. My father couldn't even remove Jerrick from the position of beta or kick him out of the pride. Our law states proof of any crime is needed."

Maddy saw a tear form then drop from Grey's amber eye. She couldn't help but curl tighter against him. She knew he was telling the truth, could feel it in her bones.

"Without Jerrick knowing, my father put a few enforcers on protection duty around your parents. He himself took a role in it. One night while he was patrolling Jerrick slipped into my parents' house and killed my mother. My father knew it was Jerrick, his scent was all over my mother's dead body. Jerrick ran afterward with his family.

"In my father's grief he half-blamed your parents for causing this and sent them away. Just after you were born my father realized what he'd done and phoned them to ask if they would return. He knew what it was like to lose a mate and he didn't want his son to lose his. Unbeknown to either my father or your parents, Jerrick had already found them, and he attacked as soon as they left their warded house. Your father fought valiantly, giving your mother time to hide you. We found her body nearly ten miles away from the church you were found in.

"My father told me he knew about you being found but chose to leave you in the system. Don't ask me why, because I don't know. I know he felt guilty about sending your parents away. He felt it was his fault they were killed. He did, however, bring the bodies of your parents home and we buried them in our cemetery."

What was she to say to that? Her mother and father had tried to protect her? They hadn't just left her because she wasn't loved or cared for? Her real parents had actually loved her? She couldn't hold back the tears from the years of pain she had experienced. They had really loved her.

Chapter 4

Grey watched the small female in his arms cry. He could smell the emotions coming off her. The pain she must have held onto all her life was now freely falling with her tears. He couldn't imagine living the life she had. To go from one home to another, to know you were left on some church step and never have your parents come forward to be claimed, and then to be kidnapped and told about your life… He could only hold his potential mate while she was in a world of pain. A sliver of anger crept through him at his father—how could he have left her and not brought her home to be protected and cared for?

Her sobbing abated and she drifted into a restless sleep. All the emotion she had gone through in a short time had worn her out. Her eyes flittered back and forth under her closed eyelids, her still damp lashes fanning out against her cheek. He had found out about her and her family from his father shortly before the old man died. He knew part of the story being his father had hunted Jerrick for years. The ex-beta was still out there. Grey knew one day the lion would come home to die—that had also been foretold by Maddy's mother.

Standing, he gently placed the sleeping woman on the couch and pulled a blanket from the back and draped it over her. He didn't know what was waiting for him when she woke, but he would try to help her and persuade her to stay. He winced, hoping he wouldn't have to keep her here against her wishes. That wasn't going to help him mate her at all. And she *was* his mate. The first time Mace had brought home a piece of her clothing after tracking her down, he knew her scent, and his cock had hardened at her sweet aroma. He had taken part in the hunt after that, so close to her and yet so far.

Looking down at her now, he knew he couldn't let her go. He bent down and pressed a light kiss to her forehead then went to the kitchen to phone Mace.

* * * *

Maddy knew she was dreaming. It was the kind of dream where you could try to change things that happened. Currently, she was flying in a field of clouds. She felt light and airy; all around her was white and fluffy. She closed her eyes and opened her arms, enjoying the floating sensation.

"Oh, sweetheart, she is as beautiful as I foresaw." The sweet, angelic voice had Maddy opening her eyes. In front of her were the two figures from the photograph Grey had shown her.

"I'm dreaming." Her words stumbled from her mouth.

"Yes, in a way, dear. When you were born your father and I gave you a little of our magic, so combined with your own you will be pretty powerful when you learn to use it. This here," the female said, gesturing around her, "is just the last lingering spell we left on you. I'm afraid it's a one-off, sweetheart. I'm sorry we couldn't do it before now, but you wouldn't have understood."

Maddy glided toward her parents, but no matter how much she tried she couldn't get within touching distance.

Her mother watched with sad eyes and shook her head slightly. "We can only talk briefly, daughter, you can't touch us as we can't you. You were named Leia at birth. Your father and I very much wanted and loved you. I'm sorry we couldn't be with you during your life, but we watched over you as often as we could. Time moves differently here." Her mother glanced at her father then looked back to Maddy. "We're glad Greyback finally found you. It was destined before you were born that you two would be mates. Don't be scared of this, sweetheart. I know you will accept it. He is a good man and will protect you with everything he has and is. If you doubt this in any way, it could hurt you both. We wanted to make sure you knew that there was never any doubt that our love for you was never-ending. Things that are seen can be changed, Leia, remember that, sometimes you have to be careful how though."

Her mother held out a pale hand as if she wanted to touch Maddy's face.

"It's time for us to go, but remember we always loved you and things can be changed if seen.

Seek out Amier, she can help with controlling your powers. She may be gruff around the edges, but she has a good heart."

Maddy watched her parents begin to fade. "Wait," she cried. "I have so much to tell you and to ask."

"We love you…" The faint, angelic, sing-song voice of her mother drifted away through the white, fluffy fog.

"I love you too," she whispered.

* * * *

After calling his beta to watch over things for a few hours, Grey sat down on the floor in front of the couch, watching over Maddy. Her scent had slowly been drifting and combining with his, making the cabin more homely. He didn't want to leave her to wake up on her own. She'd already had a rough morning.

Was it creepy to sit there watching her? He didn't care. He would be doing a lot more of it in the future.

He looked up and down her body, thinking about her luscious curves. How he would love to get his hands on them, feel the softness of her skin against his. He wanted to feel how wet she got when he was deep inside her. He had been dreaming about his mate ever since his father had first told him about her. He wanted a family, a big one. He'd been an only child, a lonely existence really. His first and best friend had been Rainy, Jerrick's daughter. When she left and his mother died he had found it hard for a while to socialize with any kid. When he hit his teens Mace had been his best friend in all things. The crap they had gotten into was unbelievable, it still made him laugh.

Her plump lips began moving as if she were talking to someone. Her small hands also began twitching, then she gave a tiny cry and her beautiful aqua eyes opened with a start.

He reached out, stroking his knuckles along her cheek. "It's okay, little one. You're safe."

Her eyes sparkled with tears as she lay there relaying her dream. "They really did love me. For the longest time I thought I wasn't loved or wanted. I barely remember my adoptive parents either, and going from home to home I forever felt unloved, and now I find out…"

She nibbled on her bottom lip. He felt like a bastard as his cock thickened, becoming uncomfortable in his jeans. She was upset, dammit. But he couldn't wait any longer, he wanted another taste of her. Lifting himself up from the floor, he leaned forward, grabbing the back of her neck, and kissed her. He groaned as her taste flooded him. He could feel her chest expand to touch his, her hard little pebbled nipples rubbing against him. He angled his head slightly to gain better access, delving his tongue inside and sliding it along hers. She moaned, her arms wrapping around his neck.

He broke away, leaving both of them panting. The scent of their combined arousals filled the air.

"Your tongue is coarser than…someone else's…" She blushed.

"Kissed many then?" He winked, watching her face turn even redder.

"Only those who kissed me first."

"Sassy, aren't you, princess?"

"You seem to bring it out in me." She smiled. "If I am to stay here to talk more, can I take a shower? It's what—about noon?"

He looked at his watch and nodded.

"I would also like to visit my parents' resting place."

"Okay. How about something to eat while we talk?"

After helping her stand and gesturing for her to go down the hallway first, he noticed her torn skirt. He sure had done a number on it. He could see her pale arse cheeks sway. That didn't help his arousal in the slightest. He wanted to find the nearest flat surface and see just how tight she really was.

Clearing his throat, he muttered, "I'll find you something to wear."

Chapter 5

Maddy stood under the shower, the water raining down on top of her, soothing her tattered nerves. With her head ducked between her hands resting on the wall, she just stood there going over everything in her mind.

Her parents loved her. It was like a record stuck on repeat in her head. That little fact made her feel better, lighter in a way. Her parents were magical. That's when other stuff started to click together. During the years of searching for anything to do with her parents she had come across the newspaper clipping of her adoptive parents' car crash. She'd survived that with only a single scratch, and yet it had killed them both. Had magic helped her then?

When she was six and living in her second foster home she remembered waking up from a dream to find her room filled with colored balls. Her foster parents had ranted and screamed at her and each other. No one knew where they had come from. She remembered several other occasions when she'd been wrought with emotion and strange things had happened, but she'd never put things together until now.

A tiny giggle came from her when she remembered an incident when a teacher had yelled at her one morning for not completing her homework. The teacher had found her desk full of live frogs later that day. Had that been magic too? That one she hoped she'd done…the miserable cow deserved it.

Maddy sighed, knowing she was going to have to face the rest of the day. Although the shower was refreshing, it was time to face whatever was on the outside of it. Thinking of the sexy male who'd kidnapped her wasn't as scary as it had been when she'd woken this morning with her laying on top of him. Her lips lifted as she wondered if tomorrow morning there might be a chance of waking up to that again.

Her mother's words ran through her head. *If you doubt this in any way, it could hurt you both.* She was beginning to believe a little more.

She dried herself with one of the huge towels hanging in the bathroom. The material rubbed against her sensitive breasts which had perked up at the thought of Grey's hands running over her body. Yes, she was willing to find out just how far this would go.

The shirt Greyback had left her slid down past her knees, drowning her. She didn't mind as long as it covered most of her. She washed her thong and bra and left them in the bathroom to dry.

Walking down the hallway, she went toward a delicious aroma wafting from the kitchen. Seeing the place was empty, she went over to the saucepan and lifted the lid. Her mouth watered as the scent from a pot of chili filled the air.

"It will be ready soon," a soft female voice said.

Maddy squeaked, dropping the lid back onto the pan haphazardly.

"Sorry, I didn't mean to startle you."

Maddy turned to see a woman about her age with a full figure and long brown hair. She had amazing eyes. They were a light blue with an inner amber color.

"Hi," she said, holding her hand out. "I'm Vista, Mace's mate."

Maddy took Vista's hand and shook it. "I'm Maddy, although from what I have found out I was named Leia when I was born." She tried to pull the shirt down as much as she could. Although the shirt came just below her knees, she felt embarrassed at being caught with virtually nothing on.

"About time he brought you home." Vista chuckled. "You are the reason my mate has been away so often, but don't worry…" She patted Maddy's hand. "When he comes home the sex is phenomenal."

"Why are you here, and where did Grey go?" She didn't think she'd been in the shower *that* long.

"Oh, he and Mace had to go off and do something, Alpha stuff." Vista rolled her eyes and checked on the pan of rice. "Mace is Grey's beta, and he's here more than he's home, so I come over and make myself useful—help out where needed, cook and clean the house, and so forth. Are you hungry?"

"Starving. It's been a long day." Maddy sighed.

"Sit down, and I'll bring it over."

She took a seat in one of the sturdy oak chairs. Vista brought over a couple of bowls of steaming chili and sat down to join her.

Maddy ate a spoonful of chili. "Oh God, this is delicious," she moaned.

"Do you cook?"

"Usually only on the weekends. During the week I often just live out of the microwave. It's easier." She shrugged, eating another spoonful.

"So has Grey told you about us and your parents?"

"Yes. It was difficult to believe at first, but then I had some kind of dream, and my parents spoke to me. You know, saying it out loud makes me sound nuts. I wouldn't believe… Do they…you really turn into lio… Holy fucking crap, you do!" Behind Vista outside the patio back doors stood two huge frigging lions.

Vista turned and looked at the lions. Standing, she went to the slightly smaller one and threw her arms around its neck and kissed its snout. "Hey, baby."

The air shimmered around the lion and suddenly the man who had been in the van stood there. She gathered he must be Mace as he grabbed hold of Vista, swung her up in his arms, and kissed her. Maddy turned her attention to the lion that still stood watching her with its sparkling amber eyes.

"Greyback," she whispered more to herself than anyone else.

His huge body was covered in golden fur, and his mane was a deeper brown. She stood and stepped forward. As she watched him swish his tail she held her hand out. Grey took a step and laid his muzzle in her hand. She could feel as well as hear the deep purr that rumbled from him. She knelt and buried her face deep into the soft fur and nuzzled him back. She smiled as a thrill ran through her. She was inches from a huge frigging lion, and it wasn't because she was lunch either.

"You are gorgeous. Oh my God, this is amazing." She ran a hand over each of his front legs in awe. "I'm freaking stroking a huge arsed lion," she muttered excitedly.

She curled her head into Grey's mane when he started snuffling at her ear. She ran her hands over his silky fur on his back as far as she could reach, feeling his fine pelt slipping through her fingers. The spell was broken when his coarse, wet tongue licked up the side of her face.

"Eww, come on, I just had a shower, thank you."

Her eyes widened as the huge lion suddenly begin to shimmer and a few seconds later a very naked and aroused Grey stood in front of her with a massive, sexy smile. His smile turned playful.

Oh shit. Quickly getting to her feet, she placed her hands in front of her to hold him off. "Don't even think it, mister."

He advanced.

"L-look, Vista made chili." She stumbled backward, hitting the dining room chair she'd left out.

He still advanced. Her body was heating with arousal at the way he was watching her, licking his lips. She wanted to nibble on them. She glanced down at his crotch. His cock tapped against his stomach as he walked, tall and proud, with a small drop of pre-cum on the end. She inwardly moaned. He looked like the lion he was stalking his prey.

"Umm, Alpha…" Vista's voice reminded them they were not alone.

Grey stopped, stiffened, and sniffed the air. He moved his lips as if counting. Reaching what looked like *three* he swiftly turned and scooped up a tiny lion cub behind him.

"Think you can hunt me, little one?" he asked gruffly. Chuckling, he then proceeded to tickle the little cub's belly.

Maddy watched in amazement as the small, golden lion cub shimmered and shifted into a blond-haired toddler. The little boy threw his arms affectionately around Grey's neck and laughed.

"I nearly caught you. I is getting better."

"Yes, your papa is teaching you well." Grey placed the lad on the floor and the boy toddled off to his mother.

The tall, sexy man with muscles on muscles turned and looked at Maddy with a this-isn't-over look before he grabbed a pair of jeans that lay over the couch. She wanted to fan her face. It was very hot all of a sudden.

Damn, it was a shame to cover such a fine piece of work.

She nearly fell over when he pulled up his jeans and there were two missing pieces of material where his butt cheeks were. Mace let out a booming laugh, followed closely by Vista. Maddy couldn't help it…she folded over in laughter too. She watched through tear-filled eyes as Grey felt around the back of his pants. Feeling nothing but his own skin, he turned, looking at her in amazement.

"It would seem your magic is getting stronger already, princess. Cheeky."

Did I do that?

After the laughter died down Tommy—Vista and Mace's cub—cried out that he was hungry, so they all sat down and ate.

"So seeing Tommy in his cub form, it seems you can shift from an early age," she said, nodding toward the toddler.

"The cubs that have Alpha in them can shift slightly earlier than those who don't. Our Tommy could shift when he was only a few months old." Mace smiled at his son, and Maddy could see just how proud he was. "It can be more of a challenge in their teens to control the beast. Grey and I often take a couple of the teens into the woods and have them challenge each other and us."

"I gather then the children are schooled amongst you?"

"Yes. In fact, Vista is one of our teachers." Grey nodded at Mace's mate. "It's important that our children are kept from main schools as they often shift not being able to control the beast inside of them yet. You can imagine the grief it would cause. We actually tend to keep on pride land mostly. Grow our own vegetables, etcetera. It's easier to stay hidden."

"Grief? Yeah, I can guess and a whole lot more. You said my father warded the place and there's another shaman now who does it, a female?"

"Yes…Amier. She lives at the edge of our land, keeping the wards going. She makes sure no humans step onto the property. If they get too close, they have a sudden urge to go home. Your father was a powerful man in his own right. The only way Jerrick could have beaten him is by taking him by surprise." Grey looked at her, and she could see sorrow in his eyes. "If anyone needs Amier's expertise, they go visit her. She does healing, fertility, charms, all kinds of stuff."

"When they found me and were looking for my parents, my picture was in the papers and on the television. Why do you think Jerrick didn't, or hasn't, come for me if I'm such a threat?" she asked Grey who had finished his meal and was sitting looking at her.

"I'm not sure. Maybe Amier can help answer that question."

"So how did you do it?" Vista asked.

"Do what?" Maddy asked in confusion.

"The butt holes." Vista chuckled.

"I have no idea. I was just thinking…" Unsure what to say, Maddy scooped up another spoonful of chili and shoved it in her mouth.

"Thinking what, princess?" Grey asked before running a tongue along his lips, a naughty grin on his face.

"Umm…it was a shame to hide your butt." She scrunched her nose up, looking down at her bowl. *Damn male asking stupid questions.*

"Well, you can certainly see it now. Talk about a chilly behind. Do you intend to do that to all his jeans?" Mace roared with laughter.

Maddy picked up her bowl and walked to the kitchen, placing it in the sink, feeling her face heating up. The main area of the house was open-planned, then there was a hallway that led off to several guest rooms. The living area was in beige and browns with a thick oak dining room table to one side. The kitchen had all the normal modern conveniences, all shiny and silver. The cooker itself was huge, double oven, eight rings. Someone liked to cook! It was placed so the person cooking could look over the house with a breakfast bar on the other side of it. Food could be cooked and pushed over to the bar without carrying it through the kitchen.

Huge hands reached around her waist. Pinning her to the sink, Grey's front pushed at her back. "It's okay. Things like this are going to happen. You'll learn."

She lowered her head. "What if I hurt someone, Grey? What if I had made someone disappear instead of your jeans?"

Grey's hands slid up her sides and cupped her shoulders, turning her around to face him. "That's what you're worried about?"

"Well, of course. What did you think?"

"That you were embarrassed you ruined my jeans,"

"No, I thought your butt looked quite nice to be honest," she said, looking up into his amber eyes with a smile.

"Can I see yours?" he asked, cupping her butt cheeks and pulling her closer toward him.

She could feel his erection against her stomach, and it made her whimper. She knew she was wet, she could feel it as it dampened her thighs.

Grey sniffed the air, and a sexy smile rose on his face. "Tell me you want me," he demanded, his voice dropping to a low, husky sound.

"I want you."

"Mace," Grey barked, not even turning around. "Dinner is over. Time to take your family home."

With that Maddy was hoisted up in the air and thrown over his shoulder with her legs flattened against his naked chest. Grey carried her down the hallway, Mace's laughter ringing in her ears.

Chapter 6

"You're being rude," Maddy admonished, looking down at the circular missing patches in the butt of Grey's jeans. Damn, it was a fine arse. She wanted to plant her teeth into the luscious cheeks. Lifting a hand, she brought it down on the bare skin, relishing the slap and feeling of her hand stinging and burning.

"You'll pay for that, princess."

"Yeah, yeah. Big brave lion man can't take a hit from little ole me," she taunted. She clenched her butt cheeks, thinking of the previous spanking he'd given her. She'd needed that she supposed, she had been so angry at the time. She wondered what it would be like to be spanked while he was hot and hard inside of her.

"Oh, baby, I have no idea what you were just thinking but…"

She found herself flying through the air and bouncing on the soft mattress she'd woken up on that morning, the mirrors glinting above her. *Geeze, has it really only been a day?*

"Keep thinking it," Grey said. "The scent of your arousal is driving me wild."

The view of herself lying amongst the beige bedding was obscured when Grey crawled over the top of her and smashed his mouth to hers. His coarse tongue slid over hers, filling her mouth. Her pussy pulsed, aching to be filled. Her clit throbbed, wanting to be touched. Her hard nipples pressed against his chest. Grey rolled his hips, pushing his erection against her core. He lifted his head, their panting breaths combining as he looked down at her. She pushed back some of his golden locks that fell over his face.

"You're going to think this is weird…" She grimaced. "I've only ever had one guy get this close before, but he never entered me. I kinda kicked him in the nuts before he had the chance. It's something that I can honestly say I have had control over all my life. I've fought hard to stay innocent."

She inhaled slowly, trying to moderate the thundering beat of her heart. At the last foster home she'd been in there had been another foster lad there, and he thought because they were both in care and no one really cared about them he stood a chance of raping her and getting away with it. Dumb shit. All he got was a case of blue balls that had nothing to do with not getting off, it was due to the humungous kick she gave them before she ran away.

A slow crook of a smile lifted Grey's lips. "Innocence, huh? You have been wondering around the house in a shirt with no underwear on all day while we had visitors."

"You know what I mean." She could feel her face heating up. "And I wouldn't have been walking around with no underwear on if you hadn't kidnapped me."

"I like you walking around virtually naked, but only in front of me in the future."

"There's to be a future?"

"If I get inside you now, princess, there *will* be one, and after that I'll be inside of you so often you'll feel lost without me."

"Oh, really?" She lifted her hips slightly, pushing against his rigid length. "Shall I let you in on another secret?"

"Do tell, princess," he answered, pushing his groin back against her.

"There has been one to enter me and deflower me, so to speak."

"Who do I have to kill?" His voice came out rumbling.

"That would be BOB," she said rather smugly.

"Bob?" He growled.

"My battery operated boyfriend." She giggled at seeing his irritation.

He growled again and nipped at her neck. "There is only me from now on, nothing enters this pussy but me." He emphasized this by again pushing his rigid length against her clit, making her breathe in through gritted teeth.

She was more than wanting him to be inside her right now. Every time she'd been approached for sex in the past she'd curled up inside. She couldn't control her life, but she sure as hell could control who she gave her body to. Even during the long years she'd spent on the street before finding Frannie she'd kept her virtue.

It had been a cold day when Maddy came across the elderly woman lying in the gutter. The poor old dear had fallen on her way home. She'd been such a tiny woman Maddy had cradled her in her arms until the ambulance had come.

A few weeks later she came across the woman again, only this time Frannie was looking for Maddy. If fairy godmothers existed, then Frannie was Maddy's. For the next few years Frannie gave Maddy a roof over her head while she went to college and worked hard, all the time helping Frannie all she could in return for her love and friendship.

When Frannie died Maddy had been devastated. Frannie had always seen the positive side to things. *Things happen for a reason* or *there's always something around the corner* were her favorite sayings. To this day, Maddy had adopted those and lived by them. If Grey was her reason and corner, then she was going to grab them by the horns and relish it.

"So, princess, will you become my mate 'til the day we die?"

"Are you proposing to me, because if you are, shouldn't you be on one knee or something?" She started to giggle but it turned into a gasp after he ground his erection against her clit. Throwing her arms around his neck, she pulled him down against her lips and kissed him lightly. "I don't know, I mean if you go wearing jeans with holes in them in certain places it will attract other women and I don't share."

Grey's eyes turned a little more amber with the black specks becoming more pronounced. "I don't share either, princess."

He leaned down and kissed her hard. She closed her eyes and relished the feeling of his tongue in her mouth again.

* * * *

Grey's cock was rock hard and painfully pushing against the zipper of his jeans. He couldn't help but grind against her; he needed to be inside his mate as soon as possible or else he was going to go off like a teen. The scent of their combined arousal was filling the air.

"Say yes," he growled down at her. "No more delays. Say yes, let me inside of you, become my mate," he begged. "Be mine!"

She looked up at him with her beautiful aqua eyes at the same time she pushed her heated cunt toward him and panted, "Yes."

Finally.

He pushed himself up off Maddy and carefully placed a finger that he'd partially shifted into a claw at the open collar of the shirt she wore. He gradually tugged it down, shredding the material. The shirt fell open, revealing a gorgeous view of her luscious, pale breasts. Lowering his head, he took one of her nipples and sucked it deeply into his mouth, rolling the stiff bud over and around his tongue. The taste of Maddy drifted over his taste buds.

He'd been sure his cock couldn't get any harder, but it proved him wrong by swelling and creating a sting of pain as it pushed against his zipper. *Fuck this.* Moving his head over to her other breast and sucking it into his mouth, he moved his hand down and tugged at the button on his jeans and opened it and tore the offending material away. He breathed a sigh of relief feeling his erection bob freely. He couldn't wait to get inside her, feel her pussy clutch his cock as he entered her. But being it was her first time—besides a fucking hard bit of plastic that vibrated—he knew he'd have to take it slow, make sure she'd remember it.

With a pop he released her breast and rolled his tongue around the nipple then blew gently on it. Maddy arched and moaned. He began to kiss his way down her body, dragging his lips over her silky skin. He could feel her trying to close her thighs, but with his body between them she didn't stand a chance.

"You can't hide from me, princess." He grinned, more to himself than her, as he continued kissing down her stomach.

"I'm not sure about this," she whimpered when he finally reached his target and licked over her lower lips up to her tiny, stiff bud. Twirling his tongue around it, he inwardly chuckled when she lifted her hips to gain more friction. Putting his hands on both of her hips, he held her down, attached his mouth around her clit, and purred, knowing it would vibrate and cause more pleasure.

"Mmm, so creamy," he purred as her taste filled his mouth. She was dripping, and it was all for him. He could feel her legs shaking as he sucked, her toes curling and uncurling over and over.

"Oh God," she panted out. "Fucking hell, make me come. Please. I can't take any more."

He winced as the fingers that were entwined in his hair tightened. Pushing two fingers inside of her and trapping her tiny, hard bud between his teeth, he lightly nipped and curled his fingers up. Her whole body froze for a few seconds, her pussy clamping around his digits. He licked, sucked, and drank the cream coming from her tight little pussy, a sense of satisfaction filling him upon hearing her call out his name in pleasure.

Chapter 7

The orgasms Maddy had gotten from either her fingers or her bunny had never been as intense as the one Grey had just given her. Her whole body felt like jelly. Looking above her at the mirrors, she watched Grey crawl up the bed after taking off his jeans. He crawled along her body like the predator he was until finally all she could see was the burning, amber, lust-filled eyes looking down at her and a silly smirk on his face.

"Good for you, princess?"

"What if I was to say no?"

She felt and heard the rumble as he growled, "Shall I go back down and start anew?"

Her pussy clenched, but with him still in between her legs she couldn't close them to get some kind of relief. "No, no more please." Maddy said something then she had never said to another living soul. "Fuck me, Grey. Fill me up and make me your mate."

A sexy smile filled his handsome face. He lowered his head and kissed around her neck, lapping occasionally at a most sensitive part. Her mind began to lose itself in a red mist of lust when a small clearing made her think.

"Condom, Grey. I'm not on anything."

"We don't pick up human diseases, so don't worry about that, and as for pregnancy…" He lowered his head again and she heard him inhale deeply while kissing her neck. "You're close but not fertile right now." When he lifted his head she could almost make out a silent plea in his eyes to let him carry on. "No matter what happens, if a cub comes along, I'll be right by your side. If, by chance, anything happens to either of us, it will always be cared for by one of the pride. I promise, Maddy."

Tears prickled her eyes. "I can't bring a child into the world and have it go through what I did, Grey."

"It will be loved and protected, I can promise that. I'm Alpha now, princess, not my father. You're home. Our cub will have a home."

"Hold on a sec." She placed her hands over his defined pecs. Forgetting what she was about to say, she stroked along his silky skin and brushed the fine dusting of hair that went down in between them. Grey cleared his throat, making her lift her eyes up to his again. "Sorry. You distracted me with your very fine body."

"Finish quickly, princess, or my cock will be entering *your very fine body*, making you forget altogether."

"You can scent if I'm fertile or not?"

Grey lowered his head, kissing and sucking, heightening her arousal again. She tried to wriggle her hips against his body to get some kind of reprieve from the constant throb of her clit.

"Yep, and a lot of your emotions too."

"So I'm not going to be able to hide much from you, huh?" She couldn't help but start to pant as he carried on licking and sucking the skin around her neck. He was driving her wild. "Please, Grey, no more. I need…" She couldn't find her words.

His cock touched the entrance to her pussy, and she whimpered. She was finally going to lose her virginity; to give it up to someone she now knew was destined to be hers. She believed that, she felt it deep in her soul. He pushed forward more. Lifting her legs, she wrapped them around his hips, pushing down on his backside. He felt huge, his cock filling her up. Pain mixed with pleasure—she didn't know one from the other as he slid inside.

Grey ducked his head down against her neck, his teeth nibbling at her skin, leaving her to see over his shoulder and above her to the huge mirror. She could see her feet pushing against his butt, his arms tense on either side of her body, his arse clenching as he pushed forward. Who would have thought seeing him fuck her would be as sensual as feeling it? She was watching her own porn movie. She bowed her back as he pumped forward, filling her totally.

"Breathe, princess, take it easy. Let me know when it's okay to move."

She felt fine. The overwhelming feeling quickly subsided and she swore she could feel his cock pulsing inside her. "Move, I'm okay."

She gasped as he pulled out, leaving her feeling a little bereft, then he slammed back in. Lifting up on his arms, he started a rhythm that had them both grunting and moaning. A fine layer of sweat covered both of their bodies. His thrusts began to get harder and faster, and she pushed against him, keeping up with his beat. A pressure built inside of her. It was nothing she had ever felt before.

"Oh God, Grey."

His mouth covered hers. His tongue slid between her lips and began fucking her mouth, keeping up with the punishing beat as he thrust in and out of her.

Pulling back, he looked deeply into her eyes. "Come, princess, accept me and be my mate."

Her body did as he asked and she came in a passion of fireworks rippling over her. He continued his momentum until she felt a second of pain as his teeth sank into her neck. Euphoria blasted through her again, only this time it seemed more intense. She felt Grey growl against her skin as he came, his teeth still firmly embedded in her. His warm seed washed her insides. As she lay feeling her heart slow she mused over the fact she'd finally given one thing away in her life she'd had control over and she didn't have the slightest regret.

* * * *

Grey lay watching his mate. He looked up at their reflection on the mirrored ceiling. One of Maddy's arms was crooked over her head, her blonde hair covering the pillow. Her other arm lay resting on his hip, her fingers moving unconsciously in a circle over his skin, making his morning woody twitch. Further down, one of her legs curled around his thigh and under his knee. The top sheet covered most of her body, making him wish he could tear it away. But knowing she'd be a little sore, he refrained, which pissed his lion off. Grey chuckled lightly when his lion roared at him in disgust. His beast would be happy to take her over and over until cubs were firmly buried in her womb. But his human half wanted to keep her to himself for a bit longer.

The mark he'd given her at the junction of her neck was clear to see. It had healed, leaving four small puncture marks. Any shifter would know from her scent that she was mated, even if the mark was covered. The memory of her blood flowing over his tongue as his fangs slipped into her skin, making her his, had him closing his eyes and taking a deep breath. She was finally his. All his. *Mine.*

He tried to relax a little and forget he was lying next to her with a raging hard-on. It didn't help when his mate shifted in her sleep, her fingers reaching out and wrapping around his cock. He had to take a breath in through gritted teeth as she firmly clasped it and started stroking up and down.

"Maddy?" he asked, sensing she was no longer asleep.

"Yes, dear?" she murmured.

"If you carry on, I'm not sure if I can keep from being inside you." He opened his eyes and looked up at the mirror to be met with beautiful aqua eyes looking back at him. Oh, and the half-crooked smile on her face too. She knew what she was doing all right.

"What's stopping you?"

He frowned. "You must be sore?"

Maddy lifted her fingers in the air and wiggled them. "I actually feel okay. I have always healed faster than normal—must be magic." She giggled.

Letting go of his dick, she rolled over on top of him, lining up her naked core directly over his groin. *Well, shit!*

"If that's how it's going to be…" He smiled. He knew she was wet as her slickness was already covering his hardness. Her heated scent began filling the air. He placed his hands on each side of her waist and lifted her with ease. "You sure, princess?"

With half-lidded eyes she nodded, giving him permission. Slowly, he lowered her onto his cock, sliding her down until he felt the top of her womb, her plump backside resting on his balls. Warily, he looked up into her eyes but only saw the same satisfaction of him being inside of her as he felt.

He stroked his hands up her sides until he reached and cupped her breasts. Each warm globe filled his palms. He moved his thumbs over her nipples, feeling them pucker and grow hard into tiny pebbles. Maddy pushed her breasts into his hands, arching her back and rolling her hips back and forth. His cock twitched deep inside her warm, wet cavern.

Tucking her legs under each of his knees and laying her hands over his chest, she lifted herself up. He had an overwhelming urge to pull her back down and thrust his hips up. Gritting his teeth, he waited for her to lower. After a few seconds her legs begin to shake but she still didn't lower. Looking up into her beautiful eyes, he saw amusement.

"Woman," he growled, his hands moving down and tightening around her waist. "If you don't move, I will roll us over, fuck you hard and fast, then spank your butt for messing around."

Her pussy tightened around his shaft even more. *Oh, she liked that, did she?* But before he could wind her up over it she dropped.

"Shit. Do that again," he begged. He was Alpha lion to a pride of thirty lions and there he was begging his mate to slide up and down on his cock.

He watched her breasts bounce as she did as he asked. She rode him, her juices rolling down his cock as she got wetter. He moved one hand lower between her damp folds to play with the bundle of nerves all rolled up in a tiny, hard bud and his other moved up to play, pinch, and roll her breast. She began moving faster, her breaths coming out in pants. A light sheen of perspiration bathed her skin. He began tapping at her clit, moving it faster as she did. The moans that came out of her mouth driving him forth.

His cock twitched and pulsed inside of her. His balls pulled up close to his body. He wanted to come so badly but wouldn't until she did. He dug his feet into the bed, pulling his legs up to thrust deep inside of her, meeting her skin to skin as she dropped down.

"Oh. Come, baby, come," he growled out. His lion roared inside his head as she tightened so hard and fast around him while calling out his name, he couldn't help but explode deep inside her.

Maddy flopped down over his chest, panting as much as he was. The reflection of tiny flickering lights caught his attention in the mirror above him. Cocking his head slightly, he tried to see exactly what was causing them.

"What the fuck?"

"Huh?" Maddy sat bolt upright then started giggling. "If you aren't doing that, it must be me."

Shaking his head just made her laugh even more. There he was lying in his bed still firmly embedded in his laughing mate and above him a tiny, silent firework display was going off.

"You'd better introduce me to Amier today," she finally said, calming down. Her soft hand stroked his cheek. "Missing jean butts and fireworks are amusing, but I think I'd better learn to do something that's constructive."

With a smile, he pulled her down and ravished her lips.

Chapter 8

They laid together for a while as their breathing and heartbeats slowed, giving Maddy some time to gather her thoughts. This had happened so quickly. She'd only been there two days.

Wow, had it really only been two days? Yesterday she woke pissed off and scrabbling across the floor; today she was sprawled across her mate's chest.

"I'd better get showered and dressed or we will never make it to Amier's." With a groan she moved off his sexy, muscled body and walked toward the bathroom. "Wanna join me?" she asked, holding a hand out.

"I wouldn't be able to keep my hands off you, so I'll make breakfast." His voice came out as a grumbled roar, his eyes filling with sexual frustration. She watched her poor, horny lion climb out of the bed, put his jeans on, and stalked off out of the bedroom.

"Pussy," she taunted, hoping he would come back in and put his paws over her. She wouldn't have minded having his hands lather her body, but she sighed, knowing there were things to be done.

She went into the bathroom and turned on the shower, then let out a yelp when she was pushed under the flowing cold water. A firm set of hands attached around her waist stopped her from slamming into the wall. She was spun around to see Grey standing before her as naked as the day he was born and fully aroused. *Shit, the man undressed fast.*

"Pussy, am I? Let me show you just how much of a pussy…cat I am." Grey knelt down before her and ran his hands up from her ankles, lifting her right leg over his shoulder.

As the water heated and rained down on them Grey held her up and gave her an explosive orgasm with his rough tongue. He then proceeded to give her another by fucking her boneless before heading off to make breakfast for them. The man was just plain talented!

* * * *

"Morning, Alph…" Mace halted just inside the front door. Inhaling deeply, a huge smile appeared on his face. "I see congratulations are in order. When are you sending people to collect her stuff?"

"What makes you think she won't be doing it?" Grey asked. He watched his beta lift an arched eyebrow and stare at him with a 'yeah, okay' smirk. "Shut up," Grey grumbled.

Mace was right, there was no way he would let Maddy off pride land now…well, not until Jerrick was found. Possessive? Yes. She was his mate, the pride's new queen. She wasn't going anywhere just yet.

"What are the plans for today, boss?" Mace asked, walking over to the breakfast bar and snagging a piece of bacon.

"I'm taking her to meet Amier. Maddy wants to start sorting her magic out."

"Okay, so want me to take care of things around here for a bit, send a couple of enforcers out to collect her stuff?"

"Stuff?"

Grey swiveled to see his mate walking toward them, her long, damp hair hanging loose down her back. He pushed a plate with a couple of fried eggs on it toward her as she sat down at the breakfast bar.

"Your bits and pieces from your apartment, we were talking about sending a couple of enforcers to go pack it up and bring it here."

What could only be classed as a wicked grin appeared on her face, and an evil glint in her eyes gave him a clue as to what would be coming next.

"Oh, you mean that place I lived before you kidnapped me and then told me about my life and the fact there are people out there that turn into animals. There are others, right? Not just lions?"

Putting the last of the bacon he was cooking onto another plate, he placed it in front of Maddy. "Yeah, there's lions and tigers and bears—"

"Oh my." Maddy giggled.

Mace let out a billowing laugh. "You didn't just go there, boss?"

Grey scowled at his beta. "Not fucking intentionally."

"What if I don't want someone else going through my stuff? What if I didn't want to move in here with you? How would you like it if someone went through your underthings?"

He growled just thinking about anyone going through her underwear or letting her move back to her apartment. He made a mental note to make sure he bought her all new underwear when he got back from Amier's. He would also inform Mace to send two enforcers who had mates, that way they wouldn't be too interested in her *underthings*.

Turning toward his mate, he said, "Eat, woman. We'll go see Amier afterward, and no more talk about not living here." Leaning down, he whispered in her ear, "I'm going to buy you all new underwear that only I have seen. What about some of those edible, crotchless things?" He pulled away and looked down at her, licking his lips.

"That's not going to stop me from going back and packing my own stuff up, *sir*. I'll compromise with you though to satisfy your ego. How about you come with me, or I go with a couple of your men? There and back in one day?"

He was just about to walk over and slap her arse and tell her no chance when pain shot up his right leg. Before even looking down he knew what it was…well, what *he* was. He'd been so distracted the little cub had not only managed to stalk him, but get close enough to climb the leg of his jeans.

Holding in a few cursed words at the little pinpricking claws digging into his skin through his jeans, he reached down and hauled the cub up. Turning him over in his arms, he tickled his small underbelly. With a tiny growled meow the cub shimmered into his beta's son.

"Got you!" Tommy giggled triumphantly, wrapping his arms around Grey's neck and rubbing his button nose along his jaw.

"Yes, you did. I'll have to be more observant from now on." Placing the toddler on the floor, he watched him totter over to his father with a proud grin on his face. Shit, his mind wasn't where it should be.

The little bugger shouldn't have been able to creep up on him.

Dropping a kiss onto his mate's head, he went to go find his boots. He was sure Mace would be reminding him of this day for the rest of his life. It *had* to be *his* son that fucking crept up on him.

After giving Mace a few orders and leaving him to it, he and Maddy walked through the woods toward Amier's. They walked along a well-worn path between the trees. The sun was streaming through the leaves, leaving patterns dancing on the floor.

"This is stunning." It was wonderful seeing the look of awe on her beautiful face.

"I guess you didn't walk in the woods much."

"Not really. It was always work or college or something else that kept me busy." Maddy walked over to a clump of daffodils growing together and bent down to inhale their aroma. "It's weird but they even smell different, fresher."

Grey smiled as she flitted from one thing to another. It was like seeing a child experiencing something for the first time. Half an hour later they came to a cabin on the edge of pride land. It was a little beaten down but the small garden out front was a picture of color. Different flowers lined a stone path that led to the front door. On one side of the garden was a stone wishing well in the middle of a luscious green lawn.

"Someone's definitely worked on the garden more than the house," Maddy said.

Grey watched her look around the garden in wonder. He'd only been there a few times himself to make sure all was well. He'd never really looked at the place as his mate was doing now. He was beginning to see things in a new light.

"Perhaps nature is her thing," Grey replied.

"Huh?"

"He means some shamans have different talents depending on what elements they chose to delve into." A tiny woman appeared from the side of the cabin. She was a little over five feet tall and had long, blonde hair down to her waist that flowed as the wind blew it. She had a heart-shaped face with plump lips and a small nose that perked at the end. She wore jeans and a tank top that showed off her tanned skin. It had been a few months since Grey had seen her. Although the woman was in her fifties she didn't look a day over thirty.

They were distant cousins; she was not only a shifter but a shaman too. That was quite rare, he did know of two others though. The woman had her quirks, like everyone. She lived at the edge of the pride and didn't enjoy too much contact with people. But Grey made sure that the pride knew she was the one protecting them. He felt what she did shouldn't be forgotten. If she fell, then the wards would fall and that could lead to disaster.

"Hi, I'm Amier." She held her hand out toward Maddy who took it and shook it lightly. "You look a lot like your mother."

"She was the one who told me to seek you out, a last spell they cast to give them one more time to talk to me. I wasn't sure if I had just dreamed the whole thing or it was true."

Amier's lips pulled into a smile and her face softened. "Your mother and father were both powerful.

They could have indeed done that. Come, let's drink some tea and I'll tell you more." Amier looked at Grey. "Thank you for bringing her, Alpha. I know you won't want to be far, but this is something she and I need to do alone. You may wait in the garden. I also know…" She smiled more brightly. "You will shift and prowl."

Nodding, he smile back at her. "It is our way, right?"

"It is," she agreed.

He watched his mate pause in the cabin doorway and glance back at him. Amier gave him a reassuring nod and walked inside. He began stripping. She would be safe with Amier, he had no doubts, but he had to be close to her. They were newly mated. His beast was already pissed at him for letting their mate out of bed, and even more so for letting her leave the fucking house. The air shimmered around him as he released his frustrated beast so he could wander about and hopefully de-stress a little.

Chapter 9

From outside the small house had looked run-down, but inside it was drastically different. It was clean and well-kept. Tiny bottles of what looked like herbs and other kinds of stuff were neatly stacked on a huge, white, wooden dresser that took up a whole wall in the kitchen. Besides the black AGA stove that sat in another corner there was only a sink and countertop fridge. In the middle of the kitchen sat an old wooden table with four chairs around it. Maddy sat opposite Amier with a glass of iced tea in front of her. She had so many questions and didn't know where to start.

"I know you have a lot to ask. I would in your place. How about you ask one question and we can go from there?"

"Why did you ask Grey to leave?"

"Because the man is an Alpha." Amier chuckled. "He would want to control the situation, maybe ask questions himself, etcetera. This is about you, my dear. Now ask another."

"My mother said to seek you out, but I…"

"You don't know me. I understand. How about I tell you a little bit about your parents?"

"Yes, please. I would love to know more about them."

"You have always followed your instincts, right? They have often led you out of dangerous situations or given you some kind of help in life?"

Maddy nodded, thinking back. The foster kid who'd nearly raped her. She'd felt something was wrong, something was coming that she had to be able to protect herself from. The time she'd been sleeping in an alley when she'd woken suddenly and her instincts had screamed at her to move. She ran out of the alley only to hear a massive boom and turned to see bricks, stone, and mortar flying everywhere. The alley she had been sleeping in was no longer there. It was just a pile of rubble and debris from a collapsed building. Another day led her down an alley to find the old woman who rescued her from the streets, Frannie Plad.

"A shaman has strong instincts. Both your parents were powerful, but in different aspects, so I would say yours would be pretty strong too. A shaman often chooses an element they can handle better than the rest. Your father, however, was one of those rare types who could conduct all of them with ease. There are four elements—fire, earth, water, and air. I myself work with the earth. I am also another rare type of shaman being I can shift too."

"Really?"

"Yes. There aren't many of us. I tend to pick up a lot of emotions, which can become quite suffocating. Sometimes it's hard to distinguish my emotions from others when there are so many people around me. That's why I live on the edge of pride land. Not only can I keep an eye on the wards, but it's a whole lot quieter. If anyone wants or needs me, they come here to me. Tranquil Hunter land is warded against humans. When they get too close, they get an urge to turn around and walk in another direction. Your father did that. I am only able to maintain it.

You, my dear, with your mother's powers too, would probably be able to do as your father did."

Maddy couldn't help the giggle that slipped from between her lips as she thought about Grey's jeans and the fireworks that morning. "Thinking back over my life, a few things have happened that couldn't be explained, and I basically ignored it. Like my adoptive parents being killed in a crash that crushed their car, and yet firemen found me inside the wreckage with only a single scratch. They called it a miracle." Feeling her face heat up, she proceeded to explain about Grey's jeans and the fireworks, which had Amier chuckling. Maddy stopped when a serious thought went through her head. "Can I hurt someone if I'm not careful?"

Amier placed a warm hand over Maddy's. "All magic can have consequences, but you can't hurt someone intentionally. If you snap a branch off and it falls on someone, it can hurt them. Or if you summon a strong wind, it could blow them over. But you can't summon any element that could kill, no matter how powerful you are. It's like an invisible wall, it just can't be done."

"Have you ever tried?" Maddy asked.

"When I was young my father encouraged it."

Maddy gasped in shock.

"Don't worry," Amier said, patting Maddy's hand. "He wanted to prove to me it wouldn't happen. He held a rabbit in front of me and told me to use each element on it. Although the poor thing got wet, dry, singed, then blown about, no real harm came to it bar a few scratches that my father healed before releasing it."

Maddy blew a breath out in a sigh of relief. "You're not going to ask me to do that, are you?"

"No." Amier chuckled. "I think you understand already."

"Please tell me about my mother."

"You look very much like her. There wasn't a bad bone in her body. She was the light in the dark. I was very fond of her. She and I grew up together. We were pretty close until she had the premonition not long after she married your father about you and Grey.

After she left pride land we never spoke. She always felt she had to protect those around her. The last time we talked she thanked me for being a good friend and said that one day her daughter would need me. She said if she kept in contact with me Jerrick would use me to get to her."

Maddy could see the grief in the woman sitting opposite her. She didn't know what to say other than "sorry" and even that felt lame.

Amier took a deep breath and then slowly grinned. "You have a mate outside who's getting rather anxious. He thinks I'm keeping you too long."

"How do you know that?"

"Scent. We shifters can scent many things about a person. Grey seems to have stopped prowling around my home and has decided to shift and is now sitting on my porch waiting for you."

"We haven't even been talking that long," she said, a little annoyed.

"It's okay, you are newly mated. Lion shifters can be pretty intense for the first few weeks. Mind you, they can be pretty excessive a lot of the time. You will learn to handle him." Amier lowered her voice to a whisper. "We are very sexual creatures, us shifters. Use it to your advantage."

Maddy smiled at the mischievous face Amier made.

"Why don't you come back tomorrow and we can start your training. Most of your magic will be connected not only to the elements but also to your emotions, hence the fireworks." Amier lifted an eyebrow in amusement. "So tomorrow I'll show you something from each element and we'll see if you are your father's daughter and can work with each one."

Chapter 10

It seemed like forever since Maddy and Amier had gone inside the house. After shifting and letting his lion out to prowl and set a few markers around, Grey had become bored. He'd heard a few murmurs and a giggle or two come from the house, but that was it. Now he was truly fed up. Yes, he could go do some work, but his mate—his new mate—was in the house behind him.

Finally, he heard two pairs of footsteps coming toward the front door. Breathing in to gather the incoming scents, he smiled. He swore every ounce of his blood sank south and engorged his cock. Her scent had changed; it was now a mixture of both his and hers, which had his lion rolling over in satisfaction. He wanted to fuck her again, make sure everyone who came within smelling distance of her knew she was his. The human half of him wanted to be with her, in her. Feel himself slide inside her heat.

He didn't think his cock could get any harder, but when he saw Maddy walk out of the door with Amier, it did. She looked beautiful. The sun licked at her skin, leaving a glow. Her eyes seemed to shine when she looked at him. When she smiled he could have come in his pants. Standing up, he walked up the steps, grabbed her around the waist, and kissed her as if he hadn't seen her for a month. He missed her taste, the feel of her soft skin. He pushed his tongue between her lips. Shit, he couldn't wait any longer.

She let out a small yelp when he bent slightly, picking her up under her knees and clasping her to his chest.

"Thanks, Amier. She will see you tomorrow, right?" he asked, not waiting for an answer. His steps grew longer and faster along the pebbled path.

"Bye, Maddy," Amier's voice drifted into the wind.

Grey ran as fast as he could, holding tight to his mate. When he reached a clearing not far from Amier's, he slowed down and pressed his lips to Maddy's.

"I want you hard and fast, princess, then I will take you slow and loving."

"Did you miss me, my lion?" she whispered, her hand stroking his cheek. "It's hard to be angry at you for being impatient when you seem so desperate."

Kneeling down and laying Maddy on the lush green grass by a small stream, Grey took her mouth again. He fucked his tongue in her mouth just like he was going to do with his cock in her cunt in a minute. Unclasping the button on his jeans, he pushed them down and freed his member, breathing a sigh of relief at the release. He ran a hand up her thigh and under the summer dress Vista had lent her. Reaching for the one and only thong she owned until her clothes arrived, he tore it from her body. She didn't need fucking panties around him.

"Hey," she whined.

He cut off what she was about to say with another mouth-punishing kiss. Running his fingers through her slick folds, he was happy to find her wet and wanting. Moving to place his shaft at her entrance, he drove up deep and hard until he was balls deep inside of her.

"Fuck." He groaned. Shit, it felt like home.

He let out a roar and began a grueling rhythm. Maddy began meeting his pace, pushing back at him, meeting his every thrust. Her hands gripped around his arms, her nails digging into his muscles. Her whimpers and moans getting louder as she neared her climax. Sweat formed on his brow as he rammed into her over and over.

"Grey." His name left her lips as she came.

Her wet, silky walls clamped tightly around his dick. It was almost painful. His balls drew up, and the tingling down his spine increased. His body momentarily stiffened as finally he jetted his cum deep inside her womb. He lapped gently at her neck where he'd nipped her with his fangs again as their hearts slowed.

"Wow, you really did miss me. I wasn't gone that long either. I think I'll leave you here when I go back and pack my apartment up, the welcome back will be—"

"I've already sent a couple of people to do that. You won't have to go back." Grey lifted his head from her neck to look at her face.

"What?" she asked, the annoyance in her tone crystal clear.

"Don't get angry," he urged. "Jerrick is still out there, and we're newly mated. I can't let you go just yet. You need clothes and all, that's why I sent someone. Please, I'm just trying to keep you safe."

"Safe? I have always taken care of myself." She began pushing at his chest, a deep frown appearing on her face.

He knew letting her go now would be a mistake. Slipping a hand around her neck and the other under her waist, he held on. "Don't fight me. Take a breath. Listen to me."

He growled, and she paused, a flash of fear flickering through her eyes momentarily, but then they softened. With a tiny nod she closed her eyes, leaning her head back on the grass and letting out a sigh.

"Will you always be so intense?" she asked in a whisper.

Kissing up her neck, then along her jaw, he reached her mouth and brushed his lips against hers. "Always at the start a male lion shifter can be rather possessive. It doesn't diminish, but we learn to control it. You are my mate, Maddy. I have waited since learning of you to finally have you in my arms. It was torture watching you go about your daily life, and that fucking toe rag you worked with…I wanted to tear him limb from limb. But I knew in the end that you would be my reward. Understand?"

She looked up at him, and he saw acceptance as it filtered through her eyes. She nodded. "No matter what happens I chose you. I accepted, right?"

"You did, and clocks don't go back, it can't be changed." He kissed her again. "You did," he repeated. "You're here. And you're mine."

He rotated his hips as his shaft again began to harden. Satisfaction roared through him when she moaned.

"Slow and easy now, princess, just like I promised."

* * * *

Over the next few weeks Grey did indeed learn to leave Maddy longer and longer by herself. He was up to about three hours now, then he'd come looking for her and fuck her silly. She swore if he kept it up she would have to walk around on bow legs. The possibility of getting pregnant had also crossed her mind. She mentioned it to Grey one morning as he was getting out of bed, and it made him smile and fuck her again. He wanted her round with his cubs. He also admitted he wanted a big family. The man was insatiable.

Her apartment had been packed up and her belongings had been delivered to the cabin. Grey had told her that the place was *theirs* now. One morning she had lain in bed gathering her senses after another night of explosive sex and she heard him grumbling in the shower. She'd gone in to find out what the problem was only to be pulled in with him.

He'd pointed to the glass shelves on the wall and said, "This is your shelf, this is mine, don't mix it up. Peaches smell fucking sexy on your skin and in your hair, but me and my lion don't appreciate going around smelling of it, thank you very much."

Of course that had led to another bout of lovemaking. Damn, that man could get it up anytime he thought of her, which was practically all the time so she was told.

Maddy had learned quite a bit from Amier on her daily visits. Grey did too, only the hard way. He woke up one morning and insisted she join him in the shower, saying he had a bone to pick with her. More like a boner.

After she heard the water start she got out of bed, gathered some clothes, and quickly dressed. Slipping her trainers on, she walked to the kitchen and sent a bit of magic in the form of a freezing spell in the water, and then she ran. Mind you, it was rather hard to run and laugh your arse off when a roar sounded through the woods. It also made it easier for Grey to pick his bone with her. She thought cold water was supposed to chill his ardor.

Maddy had also grown closer to Vista, who was at the house almost every day. Tommy was adorable, shifting back and forth from a toddler to a cub to a boy. Maddy had learned that Tommy was infatuated with Grey. Whenever her mate was around, Tommy would find a way to stalk him. Grey would let him pounce on him every now and then, but not much more than that. He was the big almighty Alpha of course.

Maddy learned that if she distracted him then Tommy managed to get him a lot more. That was until Grey realized what they were doing. Maddy was the one who received the spanking for it. However, that didn't stop her. Things at the moment were pretty good, but Maddy knew something was coming. She felt it from the pit of her stomach to the bones in her body.

Chapter 11

"I'll see you later, princess. I'll only be gone for a few hours. I don't want to do this, but I have to. You know that, right?"

Her head wouldn't move and she wanted to look around. She heard herself speak, but she hadn't even thought about talking.

"Of course I do. I have Mace and Vista here." She watched herself twist her fingers in the air, pulling four elements together and placing some kind of a protection shield around Grey. "I'm worried that this won't hold. I haven't done it before."

His hands cupped her cheeks. "I have every faith in you. But I may not need it anyway, I'm not going to give Jerrick a chance to lay a paw on me."

"I have no doubt that you can give that ex-beta a run for his money, but it's better to be safe than sorry, especially when you go against someone who likes to play dirty." With a sigh she placed a hand

over Grey's beating heart. "Go get him, cowboy. Make him pay for what he's done."

She watched Grey lean down and kiss her small but extended stomach. At first she was shocked at seeing the bump, but with all the bunny sex they had been having... She estimated she was about five, maybe six months.

She realized then that this might be a premonition, a little bit of their future?

"Look after our daughter, and try to get a nap. She kept you awake a lot last night."

Putting her hand in his long blond hair, she tugged him up to eye level. Staring into his amber eyes and trying to keep a smile off her face, she said, "It wasn't just her though, was it, Grey?"

She swore she saw a hint of red touching his cheeks when he pulled her into his arms and kissed her with a heated passion she had never felt from him before.

"Get that rest. I'll be back before you know it."

The scene blurred before her...was it the end? But as she felt a single tear fall on her cheek, clearing half the scene, she realized she was crying. She watched Grey climb into the black van he'd brought her home in and drive off with several members of his pride.

Things blurred and began changing. She was in the house talking with Vista while cutting some vegetables on the wooden board. Tommy was quietly playing with blocks in the corner when the back patio window smashed with two lions tussling together. One was blond with a dark brown mane, and the other was gray, his mane even whiter than its fur. Blood dotted both of them. Glass flew everywhere.

Vista ran and scooped up Tommy and come back to stand beside Maddy. She looked down at the pointed blade grasped in her hand, and she could feel Vista trying to pull her toward the back door of the house.

To her frustration, the scene blurred again. If these are future glimpses, at least let them play out, *she thought. The scene remained blurry until her hand*

came up to her face and cleared her eyes. She was
crying? Again?

Four pride members stood at the side of the
van looking in. They parted as she drew nearer. Inside
on the floor, partially covered in a green, bloody
blanket, was Grey. She couldn't see his amber eyes as
they were closed. His skin looked so pale and white.
She reached out to touch his skin, and it was cold as
ice. She fell to her knees and screamed.

"Grey! Oh God no, Grey."

Hands shook her. "Maddy, hey. Come on,
wake up. It's a dream."

No, he was dead, he couldn't be talking to her.
He couldn't be waking her up. "Grey?" She finally
opened her eyes to see her man next to her, his skin
pink and flushed. His amber eyes were full of panic
and fear.

* * * *

The scent of fear, and the sounds of Maddy's
screams, filled the room. At first Grey thought
someone was attacking her, but then he realized she
was still asleep, and he'd started to wake her. Once she

had opened her eyes she threw her arms around his neck and hung on like a limpet, crying "you're alive" over and over. He sat there cooing and trying to get her to calm down. Finally, when all he heard was the occasionally sob, he pried her arms from around his neck, and she curled up on his lap.

"Ready to talk, princess?"

"You died."

"I'm right here, baby. Listen to my heart, it's beating pretty fucking fast. You scared the crap out of me."

She looked up at him. Tear tracks lined her face, and she looked so miserable. Should he feel proud she had showed she loved him? She hadn't said it once yet. Did she realize herself? Mind you, he hadn't exactly said he loved her either, but he did with all his heart and soul.

"Tell me more?" he asked.

"I don't want to talk about it right now. Please don't make me." She started sobbing again.

He wouldn't push her, he hated the scent of fear and desperation on her. "Okay, princess. Just let me hold you for a while, yeah?"

She nodded against his chest, her arms looping as much as they could around his waist.

An hour later, as the sun rose in the sky, she dropped off to sleep again. He lay there and held her until the scent of fear finally dissipated.

* * * *

Maddy felt like shit. Not just shit, but unbelievable shit. This was the third evening in a row she had puked her guts up. There was no hiding it from Grey either. He was by her side, holding her hair back. She had to finally admit to herself that she could be pregnant. At first she'd been hoping it was a bug. Yesterday Vista had suggested she get a pregnancy test. Her boobs felt heavy, her nipples were ultra-sensitive, and now she was puking in the evenings.

"Morning sickness, my arse," she grumbled, getting to her feet.

Grey dropped her hair down her back and went to give her a hug.

"Back off, lion man." She pushed against his naked chest. He'd gone for a run after dinner and slipped into some silky black shorts when he returned.

She walked over to the sink, pulled out her toothbrush, and started brushing her teeth. Out of the corner of her eye she saw Grey slide something beside the bowl. A long, rectangular box with *pregnancy test* written on it.

"You'd like that, wouldn't you?" She turned, waving the toothbrush at him. Yes, he stood there with a total smirk on his face. She couldn't help but return a smile when he pulled her tightly against him.

"What you reckon? First time? Second time I had you?"

"If your head gets any bigger, you won't fit through that door." Shaking her head, she turned back around in his arms, facing the huge mirror in front of her.

"If it gets any bigger, I'll have trouble getting inside of you." He pushed his rigid cock into the cheeks of her arse, and she couldn't help the groan that escaped her lips.

Closing her eyes and taking a breath, she leaned over to spit out the toothpaste and rinse her mouth. Her nipples hardened as he rocked his hips, pushing his erection more toward her.

"Just the right height, princess." His hands crept up her body, slipping under the spaghetti straps of her top and pulling it down. He cupped and fondled her breasts, his fingers brushing against her nipples.

She hissed in through her teeth and bit down on her bottom lip to keep from crying out. It was pain mixed with pleasure. Was there ever a time this man didn't want her? She had just lost her tea down the toilet for God's sake. He leaned down, switching between nibbling and kissing her neck.

"How about you take that test?" he whispered in her ear, cooling her arousal.

Her fear and panic set in. What if she was pregnant? Would it be a girl? Would her dream come true? She'd hadn't spoken to anyone but Amier about it.

*Things that are seen can be changed, Leia,
remember that, sometimes you have to be careful how
though.* Her mother's words drifted over her.

Amier had admitted she never knew how her
mother's premonitions came to her but if she was to
become pregnant then all she could do was inform
Grey what she had seen in her dream and hope that the
decision they made was the right one. *Always follow
your instincts*, Amier had advised over and over.

Grey grabbed the top of her arms and spun her
around to face him so fast that she felt dizzy. She
looked up into his worried eyes.

"Are you going to tell me what you saw?"

"Let me take this test first," she suggested,
stroking his arms. "Then, if it comes out as I suspect, I
will."

"Why not now?" he growled. "You often scent
of fear now since that dream. I don't like it, Maddy. I
hate seeing panic in your eyes."

Leaning up on her tiptoes, she kissed his lips
while reaching for the box beside the sink. "Test." She

rattled the box, pushed her Alpha lion out of the bathroom, and locked the door.

With a sigh she pulled her panties down and sat on the toilet, opening the cardboard box.

Two minutes it said. It hadn't even been a minute when the first sign of another pink line came up on the stick. She had guessed already she might be pregnant, but these two pink lines confirmed it. There was no denying it now. She definitely had a bun in the oven.

She couldn't help the big, fat tears falling down her face. Was she happy about being pregnant? Yes. There was no other answer. She loved her lion man, he was the other half of her. The thing that brought tears to her eyes was the realization that in a few months she could lose Grey if her dream had been a premonition.

"Maddy!" Grey hammered on the bathroom door. "Open the door. I can smell your fear."

Picking up the stick, she unlocked the door, holding up the test. When she looked up at his face it was filled with love. More love than she had ever seen off of anyone in her life. Her breath whooshed from her lungs when he gathered her tightly to his chest.

"Breath…" she wheezed.

"I feel like howling. Oh my fucking God, we're going to have a cub." Grey released her and started strutting around the bedroom then stopped and let out an almighty howl. Turning toward her, his smile slid off his face. "Maddy?" he asked. "You are happy, right?"

"Yes." She smiled weakly.

"So why are you scared?" he asked, running a hand over her cheek and wiping a stray tear away.

"I think I might know a little of what's to come…"

"*No, wait!*" Grey shouted, turning toward the bedroom door.

A second later the door flew open, chards of wood spinning and firing across the room. Grey ran across the room faster than she'd ever seen him move before and stood in front of her. However, she did catch a glimpse of Mace standing there breathless with two enforcers behind him.

It would seem the cavalry had heard Grey's howl, and they had arrived, but they definitely hadn't come quietly.

Chapter 12

"Alpha?" Mace questioned.

"We're going to have a cub, and you owe me a fucking new doorframe." Grey growled.

Maddy could only stand in the one spot, feeling the heat rushing to her face. Mace, holding his hands up in surrender, stood a few steps back with a smile growing on his face.

"Congratulations, Alpha." He nodded, the other two enforcers behind him dipping their heads up and down too like Noddy dolls.

Grey roared then turned toward Maddy, checking her over from top to bottom.

"I'm fine, you oaf. It was only flying wood."

"That's Alpha oaf to you." He grasped her waist, pulling him close enough that her breasts rested against his chest. Looking down, Grey growled low, she could feel the rumble and watched as he licked his lips. His hips jutted forward, pressing his erection into her belly.

"Don't even think it, lion man. First, there's a door that needs to be repaired. Second, you need to go sort out your enforcers—"

"Ours," he interrupted.

"*Then* I will tell you about the dream that I think was a little bit more of a premonition."

"Then I get to fuck you, right?" he whispered in her ear.

Rolling her eyes and sighing, Maddy stepped from his arms and walked across the room, stepping over the splinters of wood, and headed toward the kitchen to make drinks.

* * * *

Breathing deeply, Maddy did as Amier asked. She twisted her fingers, pulling in all four elements from around her, and summoned the spell she was practicing. She was getting a whole lot quicker at doing stuff now. Cupping a ball of energy in her hands, she directed the ball toward her targets then sat back, watching the seeds grow and bloom.

It was autumn, and the leaves on the trees were turning brown and falling; the summer flowers had come and gone. Acorns and conkers fell like projectiles onto the ground from their trees, sinking into the earth to rot or flourish to become the next tree. Maddy was in Amier's garden, planting and helping nature along its way. She was currently helping the begonias flower and watching the rainbow of colors develop and expand under the cabin windows.

It was good to relax. It had been a week since she had finally filled Grey in about her dream. He had taken it in stride and promised that when the time came they would come up with a plan. The drawback was she now had four enforcers following her whenever Grey wasn't. The man went over the top sometimes, but it was fun getting him back; this morning's snowstorm in his office proved that.

"Well done. A very nice thought adding in those dahlias alongside them. Nice coloring." Amier nodded then turned to look over Maddy's shoulder, a smile growing on her face.

Looking behind her, Maddy saw the massive lion sitting on its hunches at the end of the garden path, its deep amber eyes totally focused on her.

"Aww, hello there, pussy cat. Did you feel a little cold this morning?" She chuckled. "Did you have to put your fur coat on?"

The lion stood, pounced next to her in one giant leap, and straddled her as much as it could being she was sitting down. She didn't even flinch or feel any fear, because she knew Grey would never hurt her. He nudged his face into her neck, brushing his fur over her face and chest. His rumbled purr was loud enough to hear as well as feel. Enveloping his neck and entwining her fingers into the slightly coarser hair of his mane, Maddy melted against him and purred in her own way, reciprocating his affection.

"I missed you today, my lion."

With a stronger nudge she found herself pushed back so she was lying on the green grass. The look her lion gave her from above was the look a puppy would give if it was begging.

"I love you, Greyback," she whispered for his ears only. She shocked herself admitting it to him. She was carrying his cub and they had fucked like bunnies for weeks now, but she hadn't really given him her heart. She was scared of losing him like she'd lost so many in her past. But if she did lose him, how would she feel if she never told him?

Did his lion just grin at me? She couldn't help but burst into laughter, the lion had just smiled at her!

"Oh my God, that's just too funny. One day please do that just so I can take a picture."

With a rough lick from his tongue along her neck the air shimmied above her. Where once a huge lion stood over the top of her, a now naked, muscle-bound, sexy male straddled her.

"I love hearing you laugh. It's such a sweet sound."

She stared up at him, a stray giggle hitting her every now and again.

"I love you too. I have loved you from the first time I laid eyes on you. The first time I kissed you and held you in my arms. You are my queen, my heart, and the other side of my soul." His voice lowered as he did. Their mouths clashed, their tongues fought, and arousal filled the air between them.

"Take me home, my lion."

"With pleasure."

His muscles flexed as he stood and grabbed her hand to help her up. She couldn't help but roam her fingers over his body. Suddenly the air shimmered, revealing the lion that had moments ago pounced on her.

"See y…" Maddy's vision blurred.

The world shimmered and changed.

Maddy looked around but could only see trees. She felt like she was on pride land, but she couldn't be sure. Following her instincts, she turned around to see a small group of enforcers with Grey standing not far from her. Walking over, she watched the scene unfold before her.

A sobbing woman with knotted, dirty hair knelt at Grey's feet. In fact, her whole body seemed to be caked in dried mud. The blue overalls she wore drowned her. The bottoms of her feet were red raw, blistered and cut in many places. Her pale, bony hands were held up in front of her in a pleading manner. Maddy noticed the bruised rings around the woman's wrists like she'd been bound by something for a long time.

The woman looked up at Grey, and Maddy could see her bright green eyes filled with both fear and expectation. Maddy's heart hurt with the sorrow she felt. The pain coming from the woman was significant enough to know she'd been through the wars.

Maddy looked at Grey. At first he'd looked hard and angry, but his manner slowly changed, and he bent down and pulled the woman up off the ground. Placing an arm under her legs, he lifted her into his arms and began walking, surrounded by his enforcers. Grey gave his head enforcer Leo a slight nod, and the man shimmered and shifted then toke off.

The area around Maddy began to dissolve and change.

The trees were gone, and Maddy found herself standing in her kitchen. A strange woman stood there. After staring at her a while she realized it was the woman Grey had picked up and carried. She was now a stunning brunette. She had curves in all the right places. Her brown hair was loose and flowed down to her backside. She was wearing a luminous green boob tube with a very short, bright pink skirt that showed the curves of her arse cheeks. There was a sinister twist to this scene and that was the bloody blade currently in her hand, and at her feet was a rough looking gray-haired man lying next to someone else but only a pair of legs were visible.

Before the scene had a chance to shimmer and change Maddy looked around the cabin, trying to get an idea of when this would happen. She couldn't see any kind of date anywhere, only the time on the kitchen clock, which was currently showing just past three.

The glass from the back patio doors was strewn everywhere. She gasped when she saw a lion lying prone on the floor. She briefly caught a glimpse of its chest moving up and down and breathed a sigh of relief knowing it was alive. As the scene grew dark she followed the direction of the legs on the floor to see a pink pair of trainers on the pair of feet. They were hers!

Chapter 13

"Maddy? Maddy, talk to me, princess." Grey's voice was filled with anguish.

Opening her eyes, she looked straight up into the deep amber ones of Grey's.

"Talk to me, sweetheart," he urged.

She sat up, and a glass of cold water was pushed into her hands. As she took a sip, feeling the water slip down her parched throat, the disorientation began slipping and she pulled herself together.

"I…you…a woman was kneeling at your feet, you were angry then you carried her somewhere." Looking around, she noticed she was in Amier's cabin on her couch. "Did I pass out?"

A naked Grey knelt in front of her, his hands stroking her arms. "At first you just stopped and froze, then you went limp so I carried you in here and laid you down. Amier said you were fine, just seeing something. Didn't stop me from worrying though. What did you see?"

His warm hand stroked her cheek. She looked over his shoulder to see Amier's worried face. Maddy smiled at her and gave her an infinitesimal nod, letting her know she was okay.

Taking a deep breath, she pulled everything she felt and knew about her premonition. "A woman came onto pride land. You and a few enforcers were there to greet her, so to speak. At first you were angry, but then you recognized her and took her home. There were two scenes. In the second one she was a beautiful woman, all filled out, but she had a bloody knife in her hand." She stared into Grey's worried eyes. "There were two people at her feet. One was an elderly, worn-out male. The other...I...ummm..."

"Spit it out, Maddy," Grey growled impatiently.

"I could only see a pair of feet, and she was wearing my trainers." The lung full of air she had inhaled whooshed from her lungs as Grey grabbed her and crushed her tightly against his chest.

"No, baby, it won't be you. Let's go home and go through each and every thing that happened."

With a nod they walked to the front door, saying goodbye to Amier. After Grey shifted they walked home, her hands in his mane all the way.

* * * *

Grey lay curled around his sleeping mate, his palm and fingers spread over the small but defined bump of his cub. Once they had they had arrived home Maddy had explained her premonition in detail. He had an idea who the female might be, but he didn't want to speculate this early, so he kept it to himself. However, he did put his beta and enforcers on alert.

Maddy wasn't sure when the woman would appear but she gathered from the broken patio door and lion lying on the floor that the latter part of her premonition could be the same time as before when she had seen herself and Vista in the kitchen with Tommy. Grey did mention to her that the gray-haired man on the floor could be Jerrick, but he wasn't sure.

He had so many questions. Was the woman a threat? Where the hell was that ex-beta hiding? Could all of this be changed?

Maddy stirred beside him, bringing him out of his thoughts. She began squirming, letting out the occasional moan and groan. Moving his hand higher to her waist, he pulled her back against him and held on, hoping he could wake her slowly. Tilting his head a little, he opened his mouth, placed his teeth on the nape of her neck, and growled low, making sure the rumble ran through her body. At first she stiffened, then she began to relax. This, for a lion shifter, was a move to show he was dominant, to have the submissive under him relax, giving him the control. The scent of fear began softening and scattered.

"Did you just growl at me?" she asked, her voice soft and sleepy.

"Why yes, did you feel my rumble?"

"I feel something." She wiggled her butt into his throbbing erection. The fucking muscle never seemed to go down around her. Who needed sodding Viagra when he had Maddy?

"Go back to sleep, princess. You need some rest. Unless you want to tell me about your dream?"

"It was nothing." His little minx moved her hips so her arse cheeks kept rubbing his cock up and down. His fingers rubbed over her nipples, feeling them stiffen to hard peaks. "I was just reliving what I'd seen earlier." She twisted her head toward him. "Kiss me."

Gently, he kissed her, pressing his tongue deep inside her mouth.

"Have I told you lately that I love you?" Her soft hand stroked over his cheek, he could feel the bristle from his day old whiskers as her fingertips moved over them. He couldn't help but briefly close his eyes and relish the feeling.

"You have indeed, but I will always…*always* want to hear it again." He nibbled her ear.

"I love you," she whispered.

Running his hand down her body, he grabbed just under her knee and pulled it up to her chest. "Hold your leg," he ordered. Stroking back down her inner thigh, he ran his fingers through her damp folds. "Oh, you are always so wet for me."

She inhaled deeply when he pushed two fingers inside her, his thumb tapping her clit. She began rocking her hips in earnest, her butt still swaying against his thickness. Pre-cum dripped from the end of his cock. He couldn't take any more, he needed to be inside her.

He withdrew his finger and grabbed hold of his cock, placing it at her hot, wet entrance, and pushed up. Slowly, oh so slowly, he entered her. Her body stiffened for a moment, then she began pushing back at him. He paused once he was fully embedded, relishing the feeling.

"So good," he grunted. Then he began to move. Grabbing hold of her bent knee, he ground into her hard and fast.

* * * *

Maddy wanted to bite something; the feeling of him entering her this way was so intense. He felt bigger, she felt fuller. She couldn't help but push back at him. She gripped hold of the bedding with her free hand, the other grasping her leg tightly. He pounded into her. Sweat slicked their skin. The pressure was building. She needed something…anything…

He skated his hand up her leg, stopping when he reached the apex of her thighs. Slowing his pace slightly, she felt him gather some of their combined juices up between her butt cheeks and around her anus. She gasped when he slowly entered her with a sodden finger. She came so fast it surprised her.

"Grey…oh God, Grey…Yes…"

He drove into her faster, his finger moving in time with his thrusts. She was going to come again. Her pussy walls were so tight around his cock she could feel every ridge. Finally, he roared and froze behind her after another thrust. She could feel his seed fill her insides. His hips still jerked like he was trying to push his seed in further. He lapped at her neck, making her shiver, then he relaxed with his arms wrapped around her.

"Good morning, mate," he murmured into her ear, planting a light kiss on it.

"Morning." She giggled.

Grey moaned then shouted, "Don't you fucking dare break that door again."

"Sorry, Alpha, but it's important." Mace's muffled voice came from behind the door. "Enforcers have picked up the scent of a female who has entered our land on the north side."

Grey withdrew from her, covered her up, and was across the room in seconds.

"A female scent?" He opened the door in all his glory and stood staring at his beta.

Grey had explained to Maddy that shifters weren't concerned about nakedness, but his dick must be still wet from being inside her. She wanted to duck her head and hide. With a groan she slid under the covers.

"It was mixed in with filth, but it's there," Mace replied.

"It's her, isn't it?" Maddy said, suddenly sitting up but keeping the bedding covering her as much as possible.

"Stay here, Mace. You have the house." With a brief glance back at her the air around Grey shimmered and he shifted into his lion. With an ear-shattering roar the beast ran from their bedroom and was gone.

Maddy was left staring at Mace who suddenly had a rather chagrined look on his face. He pulled the door closed, muttering about going downstairs to put the coffee on.

Chapter 14

Grey moved so fast the trees were a blur. He ran through the woods, inhaling the scents around him as he went. If the female was her, then Jerrick could be close behind. What the fuck was she doing? Why had she come back? Had Jerrick sent her as a trap? Questions clogged his mind as he ran.

Finally reaching the north boundary he came across a couple of his enforcers. He lifted his head and inhaled. There was a slight female scent. He knew their borders were constantly patrolled even with the wards, so someone wasn't doing their job properly. She had to have entered pride land ages ago for her scent to be so faint.

"Who was on patrol?" he asked after shifting.

"Hale." His head enforcer nodded to a tall, black-haired man beside him. "No one missed a beat last night or this morning, sir."

"Find her!" he ordered. His voice came out low and rumbled. He could understand how she got past the wards being she was previously pride, but fuck it, how had she got past the patrol? He would be dealing with that after he found her.

His enforcers shifted to their lions and began scanning the area. It wasn't more than ten minutes before a roar sounded. Rushing toward the sound, Grey came across a female he hadn't seen in years, and it looked like the years hadn't been kind to her.

She was kneeling in front of two enforcers in their human forms, and three others in their lion forms stood behind her. Her hair color was hard to define with the matted mud clumped in it. Her face was thin and ashen, her cheekbones jutting out. She looked like she hadn't had a bath or anything to eat in months or even been properly fed in years. She wore blue overalls that hung from her bony frame. She never once glanced up at him when he approached. Taking one last inhale, he knew for certain that this was Rainy, Jerrick's daughter.

"What brings you back to pride land?" he growled.

"Sanctuary." Her voice was weak, her eyes still firmly lowered.

"The years haven't been kind, Rainy. Why return now?"

"A mistake…one of his men made an error…Thought I was unconscious after…"

Grey could feel the pain coming from her. Tears began running through the caked mud on her face. Crouching low in front of her, he lifted her chin to look into her eyes. Although she had bright green orbs they looked dull and lifeless.

"I had nowhere to go but here. I have one request…please." Her eyes begged him from deep in her soul. With a slight nod from him she asked something that made his heart hurt, and he wondered what the hell she had to go through before accepting fate.

"Don't turn me away…kill me instead."

Subterfuge? No. The beaten and spent woman in front of him wasn't lying. He scented no deception either. Dropping her chin, he scooped her up and stood, sending all but two of his enforcers back to their beat. He then carried Rainy home.

* * * *

"You can't keep me away, Grey. I'll be okay. I promise I can help." Maddy pushed at the naked, muscled chest in front of her. He'd been blocking the bedroom door since getting back with the female in his arms. Vista and Mace were downstairs sitting with her.

"You're carrying our cub. What if something happens to you or her? I won't let you near until I know it's safe."

"Safe, huh? Safe?" she screeched. "You blockhead, I'll show you I can keep me safe."

Twisting her fingers, she called on her raging emotions and a couple of elements and sent the spell toward Grey. Her mate paled then began dancing on his very hot feet.

"You'll need to cool off, hot stuff. I'd advise a cold shower." She chuckled.

With a deep, rumbled growl he tried to grab her as he hurried toward the bathroom. She could see his indecision—endure the pain and go after her as she walked backward out of the door, or try to cool his burning feet. She couldn't or didn't want to hurt him, she'd simply pulled some hot air together under his feet, making it feel like he was walking on hot coals. Toes could be quite sensitive to pain, she knew that from stubbing them enough. But the pain would go away once he ran some cool water over his feet.

When she twisted her fingers in the air again, he turned and ran to the bathroom.

Letting out a chuckle, she went to find the others.

Both Vista and Mace turned toward Maddy as she walked into the guest bedroom.

"You shouldn't be here," Mace growled, looking over her shoulder for Grey.

"Do you want to find out how I can take care of myself like my lion just found out, or are you going to introduce me?"

With a scowl Mace introduce the cowering female sitting on the bed as Rainy.

"Jerrick's daughter?"

Mace nodded.

"Why hasn't she been helped into a shower yet?"

"We were just going to, but I didn't want to leave Vista alone with her, and my stubborn mate," he said, frowning toward Vista, "keeps asking me to leave." He growled again.

"She will be safe with me. Go stand outside the door or something. You can leave the door open and listen. Will that be okay?" she asked with fake sweetness.

Before the beta could deny her another deep growl came from behind her.

"Do that again, princess, and you will find yourself over my knee with my hand on your backside."

Twisting her head, she smiled. Shit, her man was all wet. He was standing behind her dripping glistening water drops off his delicious chest, his hair sticking to his gorgeous face.

"Promise?" she asked, licking her lips.

"Outside, Mace. She will be okay. And you…" He waggled a finger at her. "I will sort you later."

Turning around, she leaned forward, grabbed his hand, and sucked his pointed finger into her mouth. She delicately ran her tongue up and over the digit, pretending she was sucking his shaft. She lowered her gaze and watched her male's cock thicken and grow. With a smile she released the finger and turned back to the two other females in the room.

"Tease," Grey grumbled, pulling the door to.

Vista was biting her lip between her teeth, trying to hide a smile. With a shake of her head Maddy walked over and crouched in front of the shaking female.

"Hey, Rainy. My name is Maddy. I'm Grey's mate. No one is going to hurt you. We just want to help you get clean and give you a meal," she said, ducking and cocking her head to try to catch the woman's eyes. "Will you let Vista and I help you into the shower? We can sort your wounds out afterward. Yes?"

Finally lifting her head, dull green eyes looked straight at Maddy. "He isn't going to kill me?"

Maddy looked toward Vista in question.

"She asked the Alpha if he planned to send her away to kill her instead."

"Is that what you want? To die?" Maddy asked. "Because, lady, you haven't come this far to give up, have you?"

"I have nowhere to go. This is the only place I could think of to come to. It was my home once."

Maddy gave Rainy's hand a supportive squeeze and stood. The poor girl had gone through hell to get to a place she called home, even if it was to be killed at the hands of the Alpha. To Maddy that showed she had more stamina than she realized.

"Come on, let's get you cleaned up. Grey isn't going to kill or turn anyone away today," Maddy assured her.

Between the two women it took over an hour to clean the mud and gore off of Rainy. As the filth washed away it revealed old and new scars along with a variety of colored bruising. Bite marks covered her too. Both of her wrists had thick scarring where she'd been chain or tied up for long periods. There wasn't an ounce of fat on her either.

Maddy couldn't help the tears that fell, and she watched Vista do the same. Through it all, unless Rainy was asked to lift her head, she didn't take her gaze off the floor. After drying her and dressing her in some shorts and a t-shirt they gave her something to eat and drink. Rainy ate with such relish Maddy wondered when the last time was that the girl had eaten a decent meal.

The exertion of it all must have left Rainy exhausted because she curled up in a ball on the bed and fell asleep. Maddy took the time to conjure the elements and heal as much as she could before she herself found fatigued and hunger creeping in. Leaving Mace and Grey to watch over Rainy, she followed Vista to the kitchen to eat before taking a nap.

* * * *

Maddy looked pale as Grey laid a blanket over the top of her sleeping form on the couch. After eating she'd laid on the couch and fell asleep instantly. He'd asked Amier if it was wise that she had healed so many of Rainy's wounds. Amier told him to reel in his protectiveness because Maddy was stronger than he thought. But Amier wasn't standing there seeing her now, was she?

"Boss, Rainy is awake."

Grey glanced at his mate one more time and went to talk to the other female. Rainy didn't acknowledge him when he walked into the room. She was sitting on the edge of the bed with her gaze firmly rooted to a spot on the floor. She looked a hell of a lot better than she had in the woods. Her hair was clean and free of tangles, and her skin had a little pink in it.

"Rainy." He crouched down in front of her. Her face was a picture of mottled colors due to the several layers of bruising; they'd sure done a number on her. "I'm not going to kill, harm, or send you away unless you choose to be free of here, and then I'll make sure you are somewhere safe." He paused, waiting for any kind of reaction.

"I'm sorry."

"You're sorry? For what?"

"He will come. I s-shouldn't…" she began, shaking her head. "He made me do all kinds of things…his men…" There was no emotion in her voice, it was devoid of anything.

"Rainy." His voice was stern. "If he comes, he comes to die. He won't get to you. Do you trust me?"

"You should trust my lion, Rainy. He is the biggest, baddest, most annoying Alpha that I've have met." Grey listened to his mate's soft voice. The little minx must have woken and come to see what was going on. She should be resting. "He won't let your father hurt you. Shit, if he comes I have magic too. There's a whole pride behind you, girl."

For the first time Grey watched the tiny skin-and-bones woman in front of him lift her head. She looked over his shoulder. He turned and saw Maddy standing there in shorts and a t-shirt with the blanket he had laid over the top of her earlier now draped around her shoulders.

"But why? When I came here I honestly thought you would kill me or turn me away because he *was* my father."

"No, you came here because you had a tiny bead of hope deep inside of you that wished for help.

You got it, girl. Now come with me. Let's go get some cookies and ice cream, although for some reason…"

She turned her head and stared at him. "I really fancy a jar of pickles."

Maddy held out a hand. Rainy stood, walked across the room, and took it. It was the first sign of real trust she had shown. His mate was astounding. But he was still going to whip her arse later for overdoing it.

Chapter 15

Five Months Later

Over the next few months Rainy became
Maddy's shadow. She began talking and telling her
story. She told how she remembered being pushed into
her father's camper van one night. They had spent
weeks, maybe months, on the road before settling in a
remote cabin in the middle of nowhere. One night
Rainy's mother got into a fight with Jerrick, shouting
at him that she wanted to go home. Rainy had watched
her father put his hands on either side of her mother's
face and kiss her, then twist her head to the right
sharply. Releasing her, he walked away, leaving her
lifeless body to plunge to the floor in a heap.

He locked Rainy in her room that night. She
had woken to see him pounding a large metal hook
into the wall, and then he attached thick chains to it.
Rainy explained the only time she was released from
those chains was when some of the men Jerrick
gathered over the years came to her room and used

her. Twice she had gotten pregnant and both times she had been beaten until she miscarried.

She went on to tell Maddy how she managed to escape. One night one of her father's men had raped her, beating her until he thought she was unconscious. When he walked out of the room he forgot to chain her back up. She'd found not only the willpower to move but the motivation to get out of her situation. A hope that someone out there might either help her or kill her, either way she didn't want to stay where she was any longer. She'd heard from the men talking that her old friend Grey was now Alpha of the Tranquil Hunters Pride. She'd slipped out of the room, snatching a pair of overalls, and ran, not even knowing if she was heading in the right direction.

Finally reaching a garage, she'd broken in and pinched a map and food and kept running, only sleeping for a few hours at a time. She kept to as many rivers as possible, swimming or crossing them. She covered herself in mud from head to toe, trying to hide her scent. She did all she could to keep ahead of her father and his men who came after her. She tried as many tricks as she could that she remembered from the nature programs she'd loved as a kid.

Maddy told her over and over that she thought she was amazing. To have been held captive for so long and used the way she was, and then to have escaped and kept ahead of her father was incredible. But she knew Rainy had yet to accept that. One day Maddy hoped she would.

Rainy had started to put some weight on, and her cuts and bruises had disappeared—with a little help from magic. Between Amier and herself they had managed to minimize the scarring. However, Rainy still had a problem around the men; if they entered the house or came near her she would immediately look to the floor and shut down. But with Tommy it was different. She loved the little lad, and Maddy had even seen her smile a couple of times around him.

Maddy's morning sickness, or more likely evening sickness, had abated and she was often found snacking on a gherkin with a piece of ham rolled around it. She called it her own gherkham roll. Her five-month bump was growing, and so was her sexual drive. Grey was now the one being pounced on, not that he cared.

"Hey, Miss Far Away, you dreaming over there?" Amier asked, walking in from the back through the patio doors.

"Yep, thinking of pouncing, lions, and meat."

"Do I really want to know?"

"I don't think so." Maddy chuckled. "What are we doing today?"

"Where's your shadow?" Amier asked, looking around.

"She's taking a shower. Vista is going to take her on a run today as she needs to let her lion out. She was rather cranky yesterday, but her beast is getting better. It's calming down more, but it still only enjoys Vista with it when running. Grey told her at the next pride run she was to come along and try with the group. The poor girl looked terrified." Maddy wasn't sure if it was the run she was worried about or the fact Grey was talking to her.

"And where is our Alpha?"

"He's in his office. Mace came over this morning with some news he wanted to discuss."

"Morning, you two." Vista came sweeping into the kitchen, placing Tommy on the floor, and sat next to Maddy, pinching a gherkin from her plate.

"If I was a lion, I'd beat your arse right now. Pinching a pregnant woman's pickle is a crime."

Vista just sat there looking at her with a smug smile. Under the table Maddy twirled her fingers and called a spell up. Vista stopped smiling when the now frozen pickle dropped on the table with a slight thud.

"Unfair," she grumbled.

It was Maddy's turn to smile smugly.

"Morning." Rainy walked into the living area, her long, damp hair clinging to her head and shoulders. She was wearing a baggy t-shirt with some scruffy jeans.

"Now that you have curves we so have to take you shopping," Vista said, looking at Rainy.

"You would say or do anything for a shopping trip." Maddy chuckled. "But it sounds like a good idea. We haven't been for a while."

"I call shotgun." Vista moved so quick she was a blur. Tommy was scooped up in her arms and she was out the front door.

"I guess we're going now, huh?"

* * * *

Five hours later they pulled up to the cabin, the car filled to the brim with shopping bags. Four tired but happy women and one toddler climbed from the vehicle to be met by several grumpy and bad-tempered lion shifters.

"What the hell did you think heading off pride land without backup? I called you several times until I discovered your blasted phone on the kitchen counter," Grey growled, nearly shouting.

Maddy pushed through the small group of women before any of them could respond. "I love you, Greyback Hunter, but if you growl or shout at me again, you will find yourself with blue balls…hear me, sweetie?"

Grey bared his teeth at her and growled deeper. Based on the way his body was practically shaking she knew he was struggling to hold in his temper. She could see speckles of fur slip through his pores and cover his arms. She also knew he was lying about the backup. Four enforcers had been seen several times trailing them. Guilt hit her hard though, because she hadn't even thought about the threat from Jerrick until now.

"You. Went. Shopping. And had no one covering your back. What if something or someone was out there?"

Maddy walked over to her male and curled her body around his. "First of all, don't lie. We damn well know four enforcers followed us. Second, I'm sorry we didn't tell you. It was a spur-of-the-moment thing. Third, I am sorry I forgot my phone. As I said, we rushed out, but we're home safe now. And last but not least, I bought something nice for you." She plastered her puppy dog eyes and pouty lips on her face.

Grey lifted his hand up; Maddy knew it was to run it down his face in exasperation as he often did. But with a sudden blur of moving bodies she found herself pushed back behind the body of an angry Rainy who was standing in front of a stunned Grey in a fighting stance. Her were teeth bared, and she was growling deep in her throat.

"Rainy, it's okay." Maddy gently grabbed hold of the woman's shoulder to halt her from attacking.

"Rainy, don't do this," barked Grey, taking a stance and a step forward, which just made Rainy more anxious.

Maddy moved and tried to pull the other woman back. When that didn't work she slowly made her way around Rainy to stand between them both.

"Maddy!" Grey snapped, his voice now more of a rumble. He placed his hands on her shoulders and moved to push her aside. It seemed to be the final thing Rainy needed to attack.

Rainy quickly shifted, but Grey was faster. Maddy was shoved toward a growling Mace, and Grey pounced, shifting mid-leap onto a pissed off lioness. Tattered bits of clothing flew in all directions to land on the ground in rags. Rainy's beast didn't have time to fight back bar a paw swipe that missed its mark. Grey was there on top of her with his jaw around her vulnerable throat, growling.

"No, Grey," Maddy shouted. "She didn't mean it, she was protecting me."

"It needs to be done," Mace whispered in her ear.

When the lioness didn't automatically submit Grey shook his head a little and growled again. The beast went limp underneath him. After a long minute he let go of her throat, shifted, and then ordered Rainy to do the same.

Maddy shoved Mace aside and ran toward the couple. Rainy gradually shifted and knelt naked in front of Grey, visibly shaking. Maddy knelt beside her and pulled her into her arms. From the faces around her everyone was surprised, she wasn't sure if it was because Rainy had attacked the Alpha or the fact that Maddy was giving her support.

"Your heart was in the right place," she said as she pulled back to look at Rainy's face. "But Grey would never hurt me." Wariness shone in Rainy's agitated eyes. "You have trusted me up to now, right?" Maddy asked. Rainy nodded. "Then trust me now."

Rainy lowered her gaze to the ground, her whole body collapsing with her head resting on Maddy's shoulder. "I thought he was going to hit you. I'm sorry, Alpha," she said, lifting her head to look up at Grey who still had a pissed off look on his face.

"Well, that was a nice ending to a fucking good shopping trip," Vista grumbled.

A round of light chuckles filled the air. Grey growled something at Mace then leaned down to Rainy and whispered something in her ear which had her face lighting up in a huge grin. Maddy then felt herself lifted off the ground and pulled close to a heated chest. Grey put one beefy arms under her knees and one behind her back and carried her into the house and through to their bedroom.

"Thank you for whatever you said to make her smile," she said, turning her face into his chest and kissing it.

"I just told her thank you for protecting you, and that it must have taken a lot of guts."

Maddy looked up at his handsome face and raised a hand to stroke along his whiskered jaw. She loved this man with all of her soul.

Rainy had taken a stand today. She was wounded and broken but with help she was slowly coming out of her shell. Grey was right—protecting her today had taken a lot of courage. To stand up to a male, let alone an Alpha, after years of abuse was huge.

Chapter 16

Grey kicked the bedroom door shut and slowly placed Maddy on the bed. He ran his hands and gaze over her body, searching for anything out of place. She knew he was just being protective. His hands drifted over the now pronounced bump too.

"I didn't even get touched, Grey. The cub and I are okay. I can take care of myself, you know. Shall I show you?"

All she received in response was a growled grunt. When his amber eyes lifted to meet hers, she saw the worry in them.

"I won't go off again without telling you, I promise. We just up and went." She didn't want to antagonize him at the moment, because he was so wound up. She would remember in the future, she was positive of that.

Grey lowered his body, covering hers, and shoved his face into her neck. She could hear him inhaling and taking her scent into his lungs. His hands roamed up and down her body, tugging at her clothes until finally she lay naked under him. He kissed her, a deep, passion-filled kiss. Like he'd lost then found her. She couldn't help but melt in his arms and go with the flow. Her arousal grew as he laid tiny, gentle kisses over her skin.

"I need you," Grey growled.

"I know, my lion. Take your queen and show her how bad she's been."

"Hands and knees," he ordered.

She rolled over, lifting her arse in the air enticingly. She knew he could see how wet and ready she was. Without any preamble Grey placed his hard shaft at her entrance, and with one thrust he was deeply rooted inside her. He grunted loudly. She closed her eyes, relishing in the pleasure of being filled so fully. She loved his huge cock inside of her with his arms around her. He pulled almost all the way out then drove back inside her again.

"Don't." Thrust. "Disappear." Withdraw. "Again." Thrust.

His balls slapped against her clit. One of his hands gripped her hip while the other reached in front of her and began stroking her clit. She pushed back at him, meeting him thrust for thrust. The pressure was building deep inside her. He was ruthless but still restrained. His fingers on her stiff bud moved faster, pushing her to the breaking point.

"Give it to me, Grey, I'm not made of glass."

With her permission he pushed on her shoulders, lowering the top of her body, and powered inside her over and over. All of his frustration and worry leaving him with each thrust, nip, and kiss. The sounds of skin slapping skin filled the air. Her walls fluttered then clamped down on his hardness, leaving her seeing stars and calling out his name in a husky, lust-filled voice. With one final plunge Grey's roar filled her ears as his seed filled her womb. His cock swelled and jerked. She could feel his slick forehead when he leaned down and rested his head on her shoulder.

"I love you, Maddy, but if you do that again, I will tan your arse whether you're pregnant or not.

That's a threat, not a promise, princess," Grey warned her then rolled their bodies to their sides.

She curled up her back to his front and fell into a well earned sleep, knowing she was safe and things between them were okay. He might be an overprotective Alpha, but he was hers.

When she woke up at dusk, she found herself alone. Running a hand over Grey's side of the bed, it felt chilled. so she knew he'd been gone for a while. Getting up and wrapping herself in her silk robe, she followed the smell of food.

When she reached the end of the hallway she was greeted with a humble family scene. Vista was in the kitchen wrapped up in Mace's arms, trying to cook around the randy male. Rainy was sitting on the floor with a giggling Tommy who was knocking over colored blocks. Rainy was dressed in a set of her new clothes. Maddy had been surprised but pleased when she had chosen some very loud, vibrant colors. Grey was standing in the patio doorway, watching the woods.

Maddy smiled, rubbing her baby bump. This was home. She had never felt as relaxed and happy as she did now. All the past families, troubles, and life were over and done with. It had given her many hills to climb to get where she was now. It was thanks to Grey. Who would have thought being kidnapped could give her this?

"Hey, princess, how are you feeling?"

She turned to the man in question and walked across the room, straight into his waiting arms, and kissed him. "I'm good." She grinned.

"Food's up," called Vista.

Before sitting at the table she went over to Rainy and asked, "You okay?"

"I'm sorry I attacked your mate. I thought he was going to hit you."

"So you explained earlier. It's okay, I understand. I'm proud of you."

"Huh, what? Proud? Why? I attacked your mate."

Maddy smiled gratefully at her. "I'm proud because if Grey had been about to hit me, you would have stopped him. Even though he would have handed you your arse, you still tried. It takes a lot for someone to do that." She threw her arms around the brave woman and received a hug back. "You've come so far. Onward and upward, right? Now let's eat before I devour a lion." She grinned and walked them both to the table where a delicious beef stew was waiting.

The evening was spent filled with laughter and family. Maddy let it fill her heart to be stored for a bad day.

* * * *

Grey was meeting the morning sun as he stood on the porch outside the cabin with a mug of coffee in his hand. Yesterday had nearly blown his mind when he'd first learned the women had gone off without telling anyone. His enforcers were pretty fucking lucky they were on the ball and had followed them.

When he'd received a phone call saying they were entering pride land he rushed outside to meet them. He was more pleased they were back than angry, but he didn't let on. When he'd gone to run his hand down his face and Rainy had pushed Maddy behind her, he'd been startled then angry that she might think he would hurt Maddy. When he finally realized what Rainy was doing he was even more stunned.

While Maddy napped he and Rainy had sat down and chatted like old times. It seemed she needed the extra push to fully let her shields down. He had seen the difference in her that evening. It pleased him that she held no ill will toward his family.

He told her he thought of her as the sister he'd never had, and if he had known what she'd been going through, he would have rescued and protected her. He also told her she was family now, and he would make sure she never went through anything like that again. Finally, he warned her that if her so-called father did turn up, he wouldn't stop until he was dead. That seemed to please her immensely. At the end of the evening before she went to bed she even went far enough to hug him.

"Morning, boss," Mace said, walking toward him holding onto his own coffee mug.

Grey nodded. "Any news?" he asked.

"That's why I came to see you. Some of our enforcers have picked up strange lion scents about ten miles north of here."

"Are we ready?"

"Yes, boss. Patrols have been doubled. Your cabin is now patrolled constantly too, as well as Amier's."

"We need to keep the women inside today."

"Yeah, what you gonna do, ask nicely?" Mace guffawed.

He turned stern eyes to his beta, as if to say *no more joking around.* "If I have to, I'll order them. Go get Amier. Tell her trouble is coming and I need her here."

Putting his mug down on the porch, Mace nodded. He stripped, shifted to his lion, then ran off through the woods.

Ordering his mate to stay inside out of the way wasn't going to work. He knew the headstrong female would fight him all the way. Even with a cub nestling inside her she would still try to take part. There was only one way to tire that female out!

Chapter 17

Maddy was sure something was going on, but with Grey between her legs—nibbling, sucking, and tonguing—her brain wouldn't function properly. How long ago had he entered their room and taken her over and over? Her boneless body said hours, but her brain...that was a huge bowl of jelly. He'd licked and nibbled at his mark over and over. Who knew that could feel so good? She felt as if it was connected straight to her clit.

"I love your taste. Come for me, princess."

Again? "I can't," she whined. Her pussy and clit were now so sensitive it was bordering on pain.

Grey gently pinched her clit, bringing on another explosive orgasm. She arched off the bed, seeing stars. He moved to stand at the end of the bed and then pulled on her legs, sliding her down until her core hit his groin and his hard shaft was placed again at her entrance.

Looking up at the mirrors above her, she watched Grey slowly enter her. He was so hard she felt the thumping of his heartbeat, the ridges of each bump of his cock. He pushed in bit by bit, seeming to relish the feeling. The last few times he'd fucked her stupid, but this time he made love to her sweet and slow. His kisses were more gentle.

She saw and felt Grey collecting their combined juices with a finger, drawing it to her back passage. He rimmed her dark place and then slipped a finger just inside. Her muscles tightened at first, trying to keep the offending item out.

"Relax," he cooed.

He pushed deeper as she did. It felt different from being penetrated vaginally, but as he slipped in and out, building up a pace to match his own, she found it just as thrilling.

"One day I'm going to take you here," he said as he filled her tightness once again.

His strokes became faster, more intense. The pressure deep inside was building. Oh God, she couldn't come again surely. She didn't have the energy. As if reading her mind, he encouraged her and rode her harder.

"Yes, you can. One more time, princess."

Grey shifted his hips, hitting the hidden nerves inside of her, and everything tightened for a second before she was rocketed into subspace. Even as Grey followed her with a roar it seemed to come from a distance. All she could do was feel. Thinking was now definitely out of the question. She was sure if she wanted to move she couldn't. Her body felt like a boneless shell.

Grey withdrew from her and turned her over on her side. As she lay there with his seed seeping over her thighs she remembered thinking something was up and it wasn't his long length, but at the moment she couldn't care less, sleep was all she wanted right now. She would deal with her wanton lion later.

The bed bounced a little when Grey moved and climbed off it. She heard the tap running in the bathroom, and a few seconds later she felt a warm cloth wipe between her legs as he cleaned her. The bed dipped again a few seconds later, and one of his arms wrapped around her and their babe.

She managed to utter, "I know, you know" before slipping into a deep, sated sleep.

* * * *

Maddy's heartbeat slowed and her breathing evened out, and Grey knew she was finally resting. It had been an enjoyable way to keep her safe for a couple of hours. He knew he would pay for it later, but it would be worthwhile if she and their cub made it through the day unharmed. He had no doubt she could take care of herself with magic, but what if something did go wrong, or… He couldn't think about that right now.

He lay there for a few more minutes with her in his arms, knowing he was putting off the inevitable. Rainy had certainly shown she could be trusted to protect his mate if needed, but what if her father came? Would she be able to stand up to the man? Would she take his side out of fear? Would she run? So many questions he didn't have the answer to.

When he'd been on the way to wake his mate and keep her tired enough to be out of the way, Rainy had woken up and had on the clothes Maddy had predicted. *A luminous green boob tube with a very short, bright pink skirt that showed the curves of her arse cheeks.* He had nearly told her to change but carried on to his mate before she came out and saw it. Thankfully, the prediction she had about himself climbing into the van to search for Jerrick hadn't happened.

A week ago he had received news from a wolf pack about thirty miles away informing him that a group of stray lions had been seen and scented in their area but passed by with no trouble. They were heading south toward his pride. Normally, he would have headed off, taking a few enforcers with him to track them down. Remembering what Maddy had said, he hoped he'd changed things by not going.

Taking one final inhale of his mate's sweet scent, Grey slipped from their bed. He put on a pair of shorts and headed toward the living area where several lions were waiting.

"Tommy safe?" Grey asked when he walked in to see only Mace and Vista sitting together.

"We put him in preschool with the other kids like you suggested. The place is well protected. Today's the day, huh?" Mace asked, nodding toward Rainy in the kitchen.

"You told her?" Grey asked.

Mace nodded.

"Rainy," he called, turning toward Jerrick's daughter.

"Yes, Alpha."

"Can we trust you?" Grey asked gruffly.

Rainy walked over to him and knelt before his feet. "I won't let anyone hurt her, not even my father. I couldn't go back to what was after all that she and you guys have shown me. I'm not my father."

Grey placed a hand on her head and growled deeply. "You are family now, Rainy. Trust goes both ways. Trust me to make sure your father won't ever get his hands on you or another living female."

Rainy looked up at him with her bright green eyes. He saw what he needed to. She trusted him.

"Go sit with Maddy, but don't wake her."

"She's going to be mighty pissed you didn't tell her," Amier said, looking at him.

"I know, but I'll deal with that later. Mace, go see how our enforcers are doing. Vista, stay in the house but keep a listen out with Amier," he ordered.

Both females nodded their heads.

"The wards?" he asked Amier.

"Won't keep Jerrick out, because he was pride at one time. If he has other lions with him, they will have to be mentally strong to enter without permission."

"Thanks." He paused, walking over to Amier and taking her hand. "I know you don't enjoy being around others, but I'm glad you and Maddy get on as well as you do. It's been pretty nice having you around again."

"Yeah, well, you've kinda grown on me too." She shrugged.

Grey nodded and walked outside with Mace.

Chapter 18

It was quiet. Too quiet, Maddy thought, but something had disturbed her nap. As her mind became less sleepy she cursed Grey so thoroughly she would need to wash her brain out with soap let alone her mouth.

"Thatunderhandedfleabagofalionsonofabitch ahhh…" Sitting up, she threw the quilt off her and got to her feet.

A small female gasp made her realize someone else was in the room. Turning and grabbing the quilt to wrap around her, she found Rainy sitting in one of the comfy chairs in the corner.

"Where is he?" Maddy growled at the poor woman.

"Umm…"

The bedroom door flew open, on the other side was a panting Vista. "You okay?" She entered the room, her gaze searching every corner.

"You knew too?"

"Knew?" she asked, all fake innocence.

"Get out!" Maddy screamed at them both. "Let me get dressed."

"But…but I was told to…"

"I don't care. Get. Out. Before I freeze, burn, or disintegrate something." Maddy stood there knowing her face was beetroot red with anger.

She was panting through gritted teeth as she watched them slink off, pulling the bedroom door closed behind them.

"Just need a fucking swinging door on the bedroom and all will be well. More frigging people have slammed it open than leaving it closed in this place," she ranted, pulling on her silk robe and heading for the shower.

The water rained down on her, cooling her temper a little, when shock made her freeze. Looking down at herself, she smoothed her hands over her bump and measured it in her head against the one in her premonition. Rainy was wearing the boob tube and skirt! Last night she had laid out a pink summer dress along with her bedazzled trainers she loved as well.

Shit! Today was the day.

Climbing out of the shower and quickly drying herself, she hollered for Vista as she dressed.

The female warily entered her room. "Sorry, Maddy. I told Grey you would be pissed. He was just trying…"

"He's got wind of Jerrick coming, hasn't he? That's why he kept me so fucking busy this morning that left me tired."

Vista nodded. Guilt was written all over her face.

Taking a deep breath, she exhaled and sighed. "I can't be angry at you. It's not your fault he's an overprotective Alpha arse." Maddy walked over to her best friend and hugged her as much as her bump would allow. "Who else is here?" she asked as they walked to the living area.

"Me," Amier called, turning from the window she was staring out.

"Me too."

"I know you're here, plonker." Maddy chuckled at Rainy who was making a pot of tea in the kitchen. "So just us chickies then?"

"And a shed load of enforcers out there somewhere," Amier added.

Looking around for Vista's son, she asked, "Where's Tommy?"

"He's safe. Grey had all the pregnant females and the kids placed in the day care building today. He has most of the males out patrolling the borders and around the day care. The elderly are there too—well, those who aren't able to stand and fight."

"Why are we here then and not with them?"

"He didn't want to put them in more danger. Jerrick is after you. His warped brain thinks it's your entire fault for ruining me not being Grey's mate." Rainy kept her gaze on the tray she was loading with cups. Maddy didn't know what to say to that.

"So the only person who didn't know today was today was me? I'm going to kill him. Then I'll chop his balls off and fry them up for the birds." She huffed.

"Tea?" Rainy asked, setting a tray on the table, which held a pot and several cups. She had even added a jar of pickles and some slices of ham on it too.

"Thank you, and sorry." Maddy patted Rainy's hand. "I have a right to be pissed though." She nodded and rolled a gherkin up in a piece of ham and started chomping on it.

Looking at the clock, she saw it was three PM. She had slept most of the day away. That sly frigging male. Ooh, he was going to get something when he got back.

Suddenly, she jumping up, toppling the chair she was sitting on. "Help me put a block of ice in front of the patio windows," she shouted to Amier.

Amier turned from the window near the front door and gave her a questioning look.

"A lion will break through the patio windows just after three." She motioned to the big glass doors. "If we put a thick block of ice there, it will be harder to break, right?"

"I'm not sure, but we can try."

With dancing fingers they both started calling up the elements, summoning a spell. Droplets of water formed from the air to be immediately frozen in clumps, leading to one huge, thick block of ice cooling in the warm air of the cottage. Just as they were finishing, two fuzzy lion forms could be seen moving toward the house, fighting.

"Mace." Vista came to stand beside them both, white as a sheet, her mate's name slipping from her lips.

"How can you tell?" Maddy asked, pushing the other females back away from the ice and patio doors.

"I caught a glimpse through the kitchen window as they went past."

The vicious snarls and growling were hard to miss. It seemed they were actually coming from inside the house. Standing beside her friends, Maddy heard the glass shatter and wood splinter and snap. The full body of a lion could be seen sliding down the block to lie on the floor. The ice itself still stood in one huge lump, but it now had a crack down the middle. Not being able to see through it clearly, she wasn't sure which lion was currently not moving. She hoped with all her might it wasn't Mace.

Where is Grey and is he okay?

A weak but audible thump sounded at the front door, then it opened and the answer to which lion it was stood in the doorway. Vista gasped and ran toward a naked Mace who had just finished shifting. He landed in her arms. Maddy watched them engulf each other but also saw the blood Mace left behind on Vista as he did. Maddy looked at Amier, and they both walked over to the pair as they came in the house and shut the door.

"Oh God, he's bleeding," Vista cried out, taking Mace's weight as his knees buckled beneath him.

"The fucker managed to get a good swipe in across my thigh."

Between the three of them they lay Mace on the couch, belly down. There were four huge slices bleeding profusely on the back of his thigh. Vista sat by his head whispering soft, soothing words while she and Amier went to work on his wound.

"Not too much, Maddy. I can do most of it. I promised Grey I'd watch you," Amier whispered before they started.

"But…" When Amier looked down at her bump Maddy closed her mouth and nodded. Now, while a war was being fought outside, wasn't the time to fight with Amier.

"That is some fucking cool shit," Rainy declared in surprise, looking over the back of the couch.

Maddy had to admit seeing the skin and muscle knit together was pretty cool. After a nudge and nod from Amier, Maddy backed off, leaving Amier to finish up. Taking the elements from the air didn't involve much effort, but the deep concentration and energy required from herself to draw and knit everything together into the final result drew quite a bit from her.

"He actually has a nice butt." Maddy sighed dramatically, wanting to lighten the oppressing mood. "But not as nice as Grey's, his makes me want to bite it."

Vista looked at her with a frown. Her lips parted as if she were about to say something, but she stopped then started giggling, and Maddy joined in. Mace lifted himself up on his elbows, looking between them both, then shook his head.

He turned to look across the room. "What the fuck is in front of that door?"

"Ice," she announced proudly. "I asked Amier to help, hoping it would change things from what I first saw."

"Well, it certainly helped. The bastard got a lucky swipe at me, putting me down for a few precious seconds, then he took a running leap and smashed into that." He pointed at the ice. "Fucking knocked himself out." He chuckled.

"He's just knocked out?" Vista gasped.

"Don't worry." He kissed Vista's forehead. "He won't be getting up again."

Maddy asked the question that had been burning at her. "Where's Grey?"

Chapter 19

"Get behind me," Mace growled.

Jumping from the couch and shifting to his lion, Mace proceeded to prowl toward the back door. A deep, rumbled growl came from the other side of it just before it was slammed off its hinges, a huge arse gray lion riding on it as it slid across the wooden floor.

Rainy dived in front of the sofa and shifted too. Tattered luminous clothes flew in all directions, revealing her lioness. She was less blond and smaller but looked just as fierce when she started snarling, standing beside Mace.

As the door slid to a stop Maddy managed to get a good look at the uninvited lion. She could tell the lion was a lot older than any she had seen so far being its fur was mainly gray and its mane was almost a pure white. But that didn't stop it from looking fierce. Its long, discolored fangs dripped with saliva, its hair was matted and scraggly, and its eyes were a bright glowing amber. Maddy froze. Amier's hand wrapped around her wrist, trying to tug her backward. Relenting, Maddy let herself be pulled behind the sofa and watched.

Mace stood in front of it in a fighting stance, growling deeply. A huge roar had Maddy clutching her ears as another lion came dashing through the front door, breaking it off the hinges.

"Fucking hell, should have just left all the doors open, would have caused less damage," she muttered.

Looking at the second lion that had joined them, she saw with relief it was Grey. His thick tail was swishing side to side in annoyance. His shaggy mane was a deeper brown and longer than Mace's. His huge paws padded across the floor as he too stalked the other lion she guessed was Jerrick. *How did he get so close before being confronted?*

Grey briefly glanced at her as he passed, his amber eyes showing both concern and relief. Without thinking Maddy twirled her fingers and concentrated on placing a protection spell around him. Although she knew Grey was a formidable lion and wouldn't let any harm come to her or any of his pride if he could stop it, this was her way of letting him know she was there for him.

She watched the air pull tightly around Grey, Mace, and Rainy. It wouldn't stop the pain they would feel from the hits if they took any, but it would stop the majority of injuries. Just as Grey reached the pair of lions two more shaggy beasts joined Jerrick from behind through the broken doorway. Not waiting, Grey rushed forward and leaped into action.

"Move now," Vista whispered.

"What? I need to be here, I want to see."

"No, move. You have the cub to think about too." Vista was already on her feet, trying to push Maddy down the hallway.

"Vista, I can help," she pleaded. The sounds of fighting were now fierce and ear-splitting. She caught glimpses of rolling lions entwined—a flurry of blood, teeth, and paws.

"She's right," Amier cajoled. "Go. I'll stay and watch over them. If you don't," she warned, pointing a finger at her, "I'll put you to sleep and we will carry you."

"But…"

"Move," Vista ordered and pushed her down the hallway.

Clutching her stomach, Maddy walked reluctantly down the hallway and into her bedroom.

Vista shut and locked the door. "Seal the door," she ordered. "I know you can, Amier told me."

"But…"

"Now, Maddy, or I'll go get Amier to do it."

Rolling her eyes, Maddy twisted her fingers. Pulling in the air around the door, she formed an unseen glue and placed it around the door. The only way to get through the door now was by removing the entire doorframe. It wouldn't stop a lion from getting in eventually, but it would give them time to get out a window.

"This wasn't how I saw things." She paced the room back and forth, the roars coming less often.

"Your mother said things could be changed," Vista said, turning from the window looking out toward the front of the house.

"But is it for the better?" Maddy asked, exasperated at the many possibilities of what could go wrong.

"Well, Grey is here for a start, he wasn't last time."

Both of the women froze when an almighty roar sounded through the house, shaking the windows. Maddy covered her ears, trying to ward the sound off.

"Grey?" she asked the as the noise petered off.

* * * *

From what Grey had heard and could make out six had made it through the barriers. He knew one of them would be Jerrick. He didn't want to leave Maddy and the other women in the cabin, but he had to trust Mace and his enforcers while he checked on the school. Earlier in the day he had sent word for his men to gather those who were more vulnerable at the school, which was in the center of pride land. He knew even in her condition Maddy could look after herself, and with Amier they stood a better chance, but Jerrick was a sneaky bastard. Grey didn't trust him. *He* was meant to be there to protect her.

Five minutes later he did a quick check in with some of his enforcers who were guarding the area. With not a scent or sound of anything he headed back to his cabin. He ran back as fast as he could. He couldn't help feeling sick to the pit of his stomach knowing he shouldn't have left Maddy. Swiftly, he reached the cabin. Two shifters lay not far from each other. From their scents one was dead, and the other from his pride was down but not moving. They were too close to the cabin for his liking, so he pushed himself harder.

As the cabin came into view he heard a growl from inside it, and he sped up even more, rushing the front door, sending it crashing to the floor. The lion's scent hit him like a physical force. Jerrick. His gray-haired beast was standing in front of Mace, who was snapping and prancing, and a lioness who Grey recognized as Rainy. *What the fuck is she doing?* Fuck, Jerrick's beast looked like shit. Grey glanced around and saw Vista, Amier, and Maddy hiding behind the couch. He didn't smell any blood, which brought relief. Maddy's eyes were wide. *Is that a block of ice in my living room?*

He turned his head back to Jerrick, hearing and scenting two other beasts before they appeared. The lions stalked and stood behind Jerrick, backing him up. It would seem it was three on three. *Not a fair fight really. For them!*

It was time to finish this. With a leap he landed on Jerrick's back before the old man could do anything. Having the element of surprise, he dug his fangs deep into the side of the beast's neck. Blood flooded his mouth, his lion loving the taste, sending him into a frenzy, wanting more. Shaking his head and growling, he felt the pain as one of the other lions jumped on him. But the lion didn't have much time to do anything but roll over as it fell foul to Rainy. She pounced on it, ripping her teeth through its neck. He knew years of abuse fueled her blood and helped her right now. He could only hope she didn't regret it later.

Jerrick tugged enough to free himself, leaving a clump of mane fur in Grey's mouth. Shaking his head slightly, he rid himself of the crap. Grey's lion was going mental. He kept urging Grey to finish this.

Jerrick lunged, coming in low for his neck. Grey leaped up and over him, turning swiftly to bite a chunk from his hind leg. Jerrick let out a whine and roar and turned, swiping at Grey's head. However, Grey was faster, and Jerrick's claws missed their mark.

Going in for the kill, Grey rushed Jerrick. With a small amount of ramming speed he head-butted the lion, toppling it over on its side, and in he went for the neck. He dug his fangs into the vulnerable part of his neck and growled.

"Grey." Rainy came to stand beside him and confidently placed her hand on his mane. The woman had balls for sure; interrupting him wasn't a good idea at all. "Let me ask my father a question before he meets his maker."

His beast was reluctant. Fucking hell, he wanted to kill the bastard now. With a heavy sigh he rolled his eyes up to Mace who was standing in front of him, still in his lion form. Mace gave a slight nod, letting Grey know he understood what his Alpha was going to do.

Grey pulled his teeth from Jerrick's neck and waited to see if the lion would move, but he didn't. Taking a step back, Grey continued waiting. The air around Jerrick shimmered and the ex-beta appeared, although a lot older and grayer. A sad form of a man Grey once remembered fondly knelt in front of him as an enemy. He had killed his mother, gone after his mate, and made his former best friend—his own daughter's—life miserable. He had no pity for him. Grey shifted into his human form and stood in front of the man.

"Maddy's mother was right. You did come home to die. What made you think you could best me, old man?"

Nothing. Jerrick just looked down at the floor.

"Why didn't you go after Maddy until now? Answer me that at least," he growled.

"Fucking magic," Jerrick snapped. "I couldn't fucking find or get to her."

Grey looked down at the man and wondered if it was possible that Maddy's parents had managed to hide her all this time. Had he actually put her at risk by bringing her home and mating her? No, she was safe, she was his, he would spent his life making sure of that. With a shake of his head Grey looked at Rainy and nodded.

"I want to know why. Why you treated me the way you did?" Rainy swiped at a stray tear sliding down her cheek.

"You weren't her. You weren't his mate. You and that slut of his ruined my life. You were supposed to be his mate," Jerrick spat, looking up with hateful eyes at Rainy. "I was to become Alpha, but instead that fucking shaman predicted otherwise and ruined everything."

"What made you think you would become Alpha?" Grey asked. "My father already had a son who would take over."

"Not if you were to die in a fatal accident along with your father."

"All because I wasn't what you wanted?" Rainy's voice came out low. She'd gone white as a sheet and stood looking at her father as if she was seeing a ghost. "Did you ever love me?" she whispered low.

Jerrick looked away from his daughter, staying silent.

"Did you?" Rainy demanded louder, bending down and getting in his face.

Jerrick turned to face her, and with a sneer he answered, "You were a useful tool to get what I wanted, and when you weren't you were just trash to be used and taken out."

Rainy lifted her hand, shifted it into a claw, and pulled it back to strike him. Grey moved fast and caught her hand before she did, shaking his head.

"Don't." He lifted his other hand and placed a finger under her chin, lifting it so she looked into his eyes. "You've been through enough—"

He was interrupted by a warning roar from Mace. Turning around, Grey spotted the air shimmering around Jerrick. Again, Grey was faster. Pushing Rainy behind him, he shifted and pounced on the ex-beta before he fully shifted. Sinking his teeth into Jerrick's throat, he squeezed, crushing his windpipe. He could have ripped his throat out and given him a quick death, but for the years of pain he had caused the people Grey loved that wasn't good enough. Releasing the lion's throat, he stood back and watched the old man appear again, clutching at his throat and trying to gasp in breath. His eyes were wide with fear.

Grey was worried about Rainy, but she stood behind him, looking down at her father without a tear or any kind of grief. When Jerrick's final gasp fell from his lips and he lay limp on the floor Grey watched as relief flowed through her eyes. Grey sensed she knew she was finally free to live her life.

Standing back, Grey roared from the top of his lungs, letting all in his pride know that it was over—he was Alpha and victorious.

Epilogue

Drying her hands on a towel, Maddy looked up from where she stood in the kitchen over the living area. Who would have thought nearly four months ago this place looked like a bomb had been dropped on it? Each of the four doors had been broken off its hinges. As they had cleaned up she swore that glass was found in each and every corner of the large room. It hadn't taken them long to clean and fix the place back up. It was nice to have so many people come help. The Sunday after it happened, Grey reinitiated the pride potluck Sunday get-together. He had told her it had been forgotten over the years and he wanted to bring the pride closer again.

That's where they had been today. Maddy smiled. It had been a good day. Mace and Vista had announced their pregnancy, which turned the gathering into a celebration. It was nice to relax with her now huge family, but it was better to come home and be with her own.

Tossing the towel on the kitchen counter, she walked through the house, turning off the lights and heading down the hallway to the nursery where she knew Grey was with their cubs. Peeking around the door, she smiled again when she saw he was sitting in his normal place with a babe in each arm, rocking in the chair as he looked out over the woods, telling them quietly about life.

Walking over to him, she placed a kiss on his head and leaned down, stroking a finger over each of the cubs' cheeks.

"They're fine, stop fussing," he grumbled.

"If you don't put them down at some point, they are going to be forever in your arms or difficult to live with. They're six weeks old and should be sleeping in their cribs," she whispered in exasperation.

The man just wouldn't listen. Anytime their daughters cried he was there like a shot before anyone else thought about moving. At night he was often found where he was now. Knowing they wouldn't need feeding for a few hours, she placed a gentle kiss on each of their heads and went to take a shower.

Their precious bundles of joy had arrived three weeks early. Not being able to sleep one morning she had slipped out of bed and sat by the patio doors, drinking her tea while watching the snow fall. She hadn't been sitting there long when her water broke. In all the time she had been with Grey she'd never seen his lion panic as much as he did that morning. She could giggle about it now, but at the time it wasn't funny. In fact, he had been bloody annoying. Having babies at home was a done thing for shifters, this being for several reasons. Keeping their secret was the main one. Throughout her pregnancy only one baby was ever felt so when she started pushing after their first daughter came out and another appeared a fair amount of shock went through all those present.

Two baby girls were born safe and sound. The first they named Leia Holly—Holly was Grey's mother's name—and the second they named May Frannie after her mother and the lady who had once taken her in and treated her like a daughter.

Both of the babies had a shocking length of blond hair. They also shifted to their cub forms not long after they turned four weeks old, which had Grey puffing his chest out and strutting around for nearly a week.

With the noise of the shower she didn't hear the door open and close. Grey's hands slipped around her waist, and he began nibbling at his mark.

"You finally put them in their cribs then?" she asked with humor in her voice.

"I thought their mother might want some of my attention." His hands roamed up from her waist to gather her milk-filled breasts in his palms. "So much bigger." He sighed behind her, jiggering her mounds up and down and rubbing his thumbs across her nipples.

She pushed her butt back against his rigid body, feeling his erection dig between her arse cheeks, whimpering as he again nibbled on his mark.

"Today went well," he murmured.

"Yep." She panted.

Grey released one of her breasts and roamed down her body, cupping her pussy. His thumb slid between her folds and tapped against her hard bud, making her legs shake.

"Always so ready for me, princess."

She let out a small gasp as he slowly pushed the head of his penis inside her. He grasped hold of her hips, lifting them slightly as he thrust the rest of the way in. Her lion was fast, hard, and merciless as he took her to the limit and back again.

Who would have thought her life would end up being so happy?

Printed in Great Britain
by Amazon

29598042R10109